Brilliance of the Moon

SCARS OF VICTORY

FIREBIRD
WHERE FANTASY TAKES FLIGHT™

BOOKS BY LIAN HEARN

TALES OF THE OTORI

Across the Nightingale Floor
Episode One: The Sword of the Warrior
Episode Two: Journey to Inuyama

Grass for His Pillow
Episode One: Lord Fujiwara's Treasures
Episode Two: The Way Through the Snow

Brilliance of the Moon
Episode One: Battle for Maruyama
Episode Two: Scars of Victory

OTORI
CLAN

MARUYAMA
CLAN

SEISHUU
CLAN

SHIRAKAWA
CLAN

TOHAN
CLAN

TALES
OF THE
OTORI

EPISODE
2

Brilliance of the Moon

SCARS OF VICTORY

LIAN HEARN

FIREBIRD

AN IMPRINT OF PENGUIN GROUP (USA) INC.

FIREBIRD
Published by the Penguin Group
Penguin Group (USA) Inc., 345 Hudson Street, New York, New York 10014, U.S.A.
Penguin Group (Canada), 90 Eglinton Avenue East, Suite 700, Toronto, Ontario, Canada M4P 2Y3
(a division of Pearson Penguin Canada Inc.)

Registered Offices: Penguin Books Ltd, 80 Strand, London WC2R 0RL, England

This is a work of fiction. Names, characters, places, and incidents either are the product of the
author's imagination or are used fictitiously, and any resemblance to actual persons, living or dead,
business establishments, events, or locales is entirely coincidental.

The excerpt from *The Fulling Block (Kinuta)* is a Japanese No Drama,
translated and edited by Royall Tyler (Penguin Classics).

First published in the United States of America by Riverhead Books,
a member of Penguin Group (USA) Inc., 2004
Published by Firebird, an imprint of Penguin Group (USA) Inc., 2006

1 3 5 7 9 10 8 6 4 2

Copyright © Lian Hearn, 2004
Clan symbols by Jackie Aher
Calligraphy drawn by Ms. Sugiyama Kazuko
Map by Xiangyi Mo
Interview with Lian Hearn copyright © Alisa McCune and the SF Site, 2002

All rights reserved

THE LIBRARY OF CONGRESS HAS CATALOGUED THE RIVERHEAD EDITION AS FOLLOWS:
Hearn, Lian.
Brilliance of the moon / Lian Hearn
p. cm.—(Tales of the Otori , bk. 3)
ISBN 1-57322-270-4
1. Inheritance and succession—Fiction. 2. Married people—Fiction.
3. Revenge—Fiction. 4. Japan—Fiction. I. Title.
PR9619.3.H3725B75 2004 2003061777
823'.914—dc21

ISBN 0-14-240594-9

Printed in China

To B.

FOREWORD

These events took place in the months following the marriage of Otori Takeo and Shirakawa Kaede at the temple at Terayama. This marriage strengthened Kaede's resolve to inherit the domain of Maruyama and gave Takeo the resources he needed to carry out his work of revenge for his adopted father Shigeru and take his place as head of the Otori clan. However, it also enraged Arai Daiichi, the warlord who now controlled most of the Three Countries, and insulted the nobleman Lord Fujiwara, who considered Kaede betrothed to him.

The previous winter, Takeo, under the Tribe's sentence of death, had fled to Terayama, where the detailed records of the Tribe that Shigeru had compiled were given to him, along with the Otori sword Jato. On the way, his life was saved by the outcast Jo-An, one of the forbidden sect, the Hidden, who took him to a mountain shrine to hear the prophetic words of a holy woman.

Three bloods are mixed in you. You were born into the Hidden, but your life has been brought into the open and is no longer your own. Earth will deliver what heaven desires.

Your lands will stretch from sea to sea, but peace comes at the price of bloodshed. Five battles will buy you peace, four to win and one to lose. . . .

THE THREE COUNTRIES

N 北

MATSUE

THE EAST

東 Tohan

AWA

INUYAMA

Hinode

Mino

————— *fief boundaries*

.... *fief boundaries*
before Yaegahara

— — — — *high road*

  battlefields

  castletown

  shrine

  temple

CHARACTERS

The Clans

THE OTORI
(Middle Country; castletown: Hagi)

Otori Shigeru: rightful heir to the clan
Otori Takeshi: his younger brother, murdered by the Tohan clan **(d.)**
Otori Takeo: (born Tomasu) his adopted son
Otori Shigemori: Shigeru's father, killed at the battle of Yaegahara **(d.)**
Otori Ichiro: a distant relative, Shigeru and Takeo's teacher

Chiyo
Haruka: maids in the household

Shiro: a carpenter

Otori Shoichi: Shigeru's uncle, now lord of the clan
Otori Masahiro: Shoichi's younger brother
Otori Yoshitomi: Masahiro's son

Miyoshi Kahei: brothers, friends of Takeo
Miyoshi Gemba

Miyoshi Satoru: their father, captain of the guard in Hagi castle

Endo Chikara: a senior retainer

Terada Fumifusa: a pirate
Terada Fumio: his son, friend of Takeo

Ryoma: a fisherman, Masahiro's illegitimate son

THE TOHAN
(The East; castletown: Inuyama)

Iida Sadamu: lord of the clan
Iida Nariaki: Sadamu's cousin

Ando, Abe: Iida's retainers

Lord Noguchi: an ally
Lady Noguchi: his wife
Junko: a servant in Noguchi castle

THE SEISHUU
*(An alliance of several ancient families in the West;
main castletowns: Kumamoto and Maruyama)*

Arai Daiichi: a warlord

Niwa Satoru: a retainer
Akita Tsutomu: a retainer
Sonoda Mitsuru: Akita's nephew
Maruyama Naomi: head of the Maruyama domain,
   Shigeru's lover

Mariko: her daughter
Sachie: her maid

Sugita Haruki: a retainer
Sugita Hiroshi: his nephew
Sakai Masaki: Hiroshi's cousin

Lord Shirakawa
Kaede: Shirakawa's eldest daughter, Lady Maruyama's cousin
Ai, Hana: Shirakawa's daughters

Ayame
Manami
Akane: maids in the household

Amano Tenzo: a Shirakawa retainer

Shoji Kiyoshi: senior retainer to Lord Shirakawa

The Tribe

THE MUTO FAMILY

Muto Kenji: Takeo's teacher, the master
Muto Shizuka: Kenji's niece, Arai's mistress, and Kaede's
    companion
Dr. Ishida: his physician
Zenko, Taku: her sons
Muto Seiko: Kenji's wife
Muto Yuki: their daughter
Muto Yuzuru: a cousin

Kana
Miyabi: maids

THE KIKUTA FAMILY

Kikuta Isamu: Takeo's real father (**d.**)
Kikuta Kotaro: his cousin, the Master
Kikuta Gosaburo: Kotaro's younger brother
Kikuta Akio: their nephew
Kikuta Hajime: a wrestler
Sadako: a maid

THE KURODA FAMILY

Kuroda Shintaro: a famous assassin
Kondo Kiichi
Imai Kazuo
Kudo Keiko

Others

Lord Fujiwara: a nobleman, exiled from the capital
Mamoru: his protégé and companion
Ono Rieko: his cousin
Murita: a retainer

Matsuda Shingen: the abbot at Terayama
Kubo Makoto: a monk, Takeo's closest friend

Jin-emon: a bandit

Jiro: a farmer's son

Jo-An: an outcast

Horses

Raku: gray with black mane and tail, Takeo's first horse, given
   by him to Kaede
Kyu: black, Shigeru's horse, disappeared in Inuyama
Aoi: black, half brother to Kyu
Ki: Amano's chestnut
Shun: Takeo's bay, a very clever horse

bold = main characters
(d.) = character died before the start of *Across the Nightingale Floor,*
   Episode 1

シテ　音づれの、稀なる中の秋風に、

地　夏をも待たで、枯るる夕べかな。

シテ　遠里人も眺むらん、

地　誰が夜を秋と月にしも訪れじ。

地　面白の折からや。哀れ、秋の夕方、

地　牡鹿の声も心凄く、見ぬ山風を

地　送り来て、梢はいづれと葉

地　散る、空すさまじき月影の

シテ　軒の忍に映ろひて、

シテ　露の玉世れかる身の、

地　思ひを述ぶる夜すがらかな。

地　宮漏高く立つて、風北に巡り。

シテ　隣の砧緩く急いで、月西に流る。

世阿弥作「砧」より

Others too, in far-flung villages,

Will no doubt be gazing at this moon

That never asks which watcher claims the night . . .

Loud on the unseen mountain wind,

A stag's cry quivers in the heart,

And somewhere a twig lets one leaf fall.

ZEAMI, *THE FULLING BLOCK (KINUTA)*

Brilliance of the Moon

SCARS OF VICTORY

·1·

When Takeo left for the coast, and the Miyoshi
brothers for Inuyama, Kaede saw the excitement
and anticipation on their faces and was filled with resentment at being left behind. In the days that followed she
was plagued by fears and anxieties. She missed her
husband's physical presence more than she would have
thought possible; she was jealous of Makoto being allowed
to accompany him when she was not; she feared for Takeo's
safety and was angry with him at the same time.

His quest for revenge is more important to him than I am, she
thought often. *Did he marry me just to further his plans of revenge?*
She believed he loved her deeply, but he was a man, a warrior,

and if he had to choose, she knew he would choose revenge. *I would be the same if I were a man,* she told herself. *I cannot even give him a child: What use am I as a woman? I should have been born a man. May I be allowed to return as one!*

She told no one of these thoughts. Indeed, there was no one in whom she could confide. Sugita and the other elders were polite, even affectionate, to her but seemed to avoid her company. She kept herself busy all day, overseeing the household, riding out with Amano, and making copies of the records that Takeo had entrusted to her. After the attempted theft she'd thought it would be a wise precaution and she hoped it would help her understand the ferocity of Takeo's campaign against the Tribe and the anguish it had caused him. She herself had been disturbed by the slaughter, and also by the piles of dead after the battle at Asagawa. It took so long to raise a man, and life was extinguished so easily. She feared retribution, both from the living and from the dead. Yet what else could Takeo do when so many were conspiring to kill him?

She, too, had killed, had had men killed on her orders: Had losing her child been punishment for her own actions? Her desires were changing; now she was moved to protect and to nurture, to create life, not to destroy it. Was it possible to hold on to her domain and rule it without violence? She had many hours of solitude to think about these things.

Takeo had said he would be back within a week; the time passed, he did not return, and her anxiety grew. There were plans and decisions that needed to be made about the domain's future, but the elders continued to be evasive, and every suggestion she made to Sugita was greeted by a deep bow and the advice to wait until her husband returned. Twice she tried to summon the elders for a council meeting, but one by one they pleaded indisposition.

"It's remarkable that everyone is sick on the same day," she said tartly to Sugita. "I had no idea that Maruyama was so unhealthy for old people."

"Be patient, Lady Kaede," he said. "Nothing needs to be decided before Lord Takeo's return, and that will be any day now. He may have urgent commands for the men; they must be kept in readiness for him. All we can do is wait for him."

Her irritation was compounded by the realization that, even though it was her domain, everyone still deferred to Takeo. He was her husband and she must defer to him, too; yet Maruyama and Shirakawa were hers and she should be able to act in them as she wished. Part of her was shocked that Takeo had gone to make an alliance with pirates. It was like his association with outcasts and farmers: There was something unnatural about it. She thought it must all come from being born into the Hidden. This knowledge that he had shared with her both attracted and repelled her. All the rules of her class told her that her blood was purer than his and that by birth she was of higher rank. She was ashamed of this feeling and tried to suppress it, but it niggled at her and the longer he was away, the more insistent it became.

"Where is your nephew?" she said to Sugita, wanting distraction. "Send him to me. Let me look at someone under the age of thirty!"

Hiroshi was hardly better company, equally resentful at being left behind. He had hoped to go to Inuyama with Kahei and Gemba.

"They don't even know the road," he grumbled. "I would have shown them everything. I have to stay here and study with my uncle. Even Jiro was allowed to go with Lord Otori."

"Jiro is much older than you," Kaede said.

"Only five years. And he's the one who should be studying. I already know far more letters than he does."

"That's because you started earlier. You should never despise people because they haven't had your opportunities." She studied him; he was a little small for his age, but strong and well put together; he would be a handsome man. "You are about the same age as my sister," she said.

"Does your sister look like you?"

"People say so. I think she is more beautiful."

"That couldn't be possible," he said quickly, making her laugh. His face colored slightly. "Everyone says Lady Otori is the most beautiful woman in the Three Countries."

"What have they seen?" she retorted. "In the capital, in the emperor's court, there are women so lovely men's eyes shrivel up when they look at them. They are kept behind screens lest the whole court go blind."

"What do their husbands do?" he said doubtfully.

"They have to wear blindfolds," she teased, and threw a cloth that lay next to her over his head. She held him playfully for a few moments, then he twisted away from her. She saw he was ruffled; she had treated him like a child and he wanted to be a man.

"Girls are lucky: They don't have to study," he said.

"But my sister loves to study and so do I. Girls should

learn to read and write just the same as boys. Then they can help their husbands, as I am helping mine."

"Most people have scribes to do that sort of thing, especially if they can't write themselves."

"My husband can write," she said swiftly, "but like Jiro he started learning later than you."

Hiroshi looked horrified. "I didn't mean to say anything against him! Lord Otori saved my life and revenged my father's death. I owe everything to him, but . . ."

"But what?" she prompted, uncomfortably aware of some shadow of disloyalty.

"I'm only telling you what people say," Hiroshi said. "They say he is strange. He mixes with outcasts; he lets farmers fight; he has started a campaign against certain merchants that no one understands. They say he cannot have been brought up as a warrior, and they wonder what his upbringing was."

"Who says it? The townspeople?"

"No, people like my family."

"Maruyama warriors?"

"Yes, and some say he is a sorcerer."

She could hardly be surprised; these were exactly the

things that worried her about Takeo; yet she was outraged that her warriors should be so disloyal to him.

"Maybe his upbringing was a little unusual," she said, "but he is heir to the Otori clan by blood and by adoption, as well as being my husband. No one has the right to say anything against him." She would find out who it was and have them silenced. "You must be my spy," she said to Hiroshi. "Report to me anyone who gives the slightest sign of disloyalty."

After that, Hiroshi came to her every day, showed her what he had learned in his studies, and told her what he heard among the warrior class. It was nothing definite, just whispers, sometimes jokes, maybe no more than the idle chatter of men with not enough to occupy themselves. She resolved to do nothing about it for the time being but to warn Takeo when he returned.

The time of the great heat began, and it was too sultry to ride outside. Since Kaede could take no decisions till Takeo's return, and since she expected him every day, she spent most of her time kneeling at the lacquer writing table, copying the Tribe records. The doors to the residence were all opened to catch the least breeze, and the sound of insects was deafening. Her preferred room looked out over pools and a waterfall; through the azalea bushes she could see the silver-weathered tea house. Every day she promised herself that she would make tea there for Takeo that night, and every day she was disappointed. Sometimes kingfishers came to the pools and the flash of blue and orange would distract her momentarily. Once a heron alighted outside the veranda and she thought it was a sign that he would be back that day, but he did not come.

She let no one see what she was writing, for she quickly realized the importance of the records. She was amazed at what Shigeru had uncovered, and wondered if someone within the Tribe had acted as his informant. She concealed the original records and the copies in a different place every night and tried to commit as much as possible to memory. She became obsessed with the idea of the secret network, watched for signs of them everywhere, trusted no one, even though Takeo's first work at Maruyama had been to purge the castle household. The range of the Tribe daunted her; she did not see how Takeo would ever escape them. Then the thought would come to her that they had already caught up with him—that he was lying dead somewhere and she would never see him again.

He was right, she thought. *They must all be killed; they must be rooted out, for they seek to destroy him. And if they destroy him, they destroy me.*

The faces of Shizuka and Muto Kenji often rose before her mind's eye. She regretted the trust she had placed in Shizuka and wondered how much of Kaede's life her companion had revealed to others in the Tribe. She had thought that both Shizuka and Kenji had been fond of her; had all that affection been feigned? They had nearly died together in Inuyama Castle; did that count for nothing? She felt betrayed by Shizuka, but at the same time she missed her badly and wished she had someone like her to confide in.

Her monthly bleeding came, bringing her renewed disappointment and placing her in seclusion for a week. Not even Hiroshi visited her. When it was over the copying was finished, too, and she became even more restless. The Festival of the Dead came and went, leaving her filled with sorrow and regrets for the departed. The work on the residence that had gone on all summer was completed, and the rooms looked beautiful, but they felt empty and unlived in. Hiroshi asked one morning, "Why isn't your sister here with you?" and on a sudden impulse she said, "Shall we ride to my house and fetch her?"

There had been a week of leaden skies, as if a typhoon

were threatening, but then the weather had suddenly cleared and the heat had abated a little. The nights were cooler and it seemed a perfect time to travel. Sugita tried to dissuade her, and even the elusive elders appeared one by one to argue against it, but she ignored them. Shirakawa was only two or three days away. If Takeo came home before she returned, he might ride and join her. And the journey would stop her from fretting all day long.

"We can send for your sisters," Sugita said. "It is an excellent idea; I should have thought of it myself. I will go to escort them."

"I need to see my household," she replied. Now that the idea was in her head, she could not relinquish it. "I have not spoken to my men since my marriage. I should have gone weeks ago. I must check on my land and see that the harvest will be brought in."

She did not tell Sugita, but she had another reason for the journey, one that had lain in her mind all summer. She would go to the sacred caves of the Shirakawa, drink the river's elemental water, and pray to the goddess for a child.

"I will be away only a few days."

"I am afraid your husband will not approve."

"He trusts my judgment in all things," she replied. "And, after all, didn't Lady Naomi often travel alone?"

Because he was accustomed to receiving orders from a woman, she was able to overcome his misgivings. She chose Amano to go with her, as well as a few of her own men who had accompanied her since she had left in the spring for Terayama. After some consideration she took none of her women with her, not even Manami. She wanted to go quickly, on horseback, without the formalities and dignity that she would have to put up with if she traveled openly. Manami pleaded and then sulked, but Kaede was adamant.

She rode Raku, refusing even to take a palanquin with her. Before she left she had planned to hide the copies of the records below the floor of the tea room, but the hints of disloyalty still worried her, and in the end she could not bear to leave them where anyone might find them. She decided to take both sets with her, already thinking she might hide the originals somewhere in her house at Shirakawa. After much pleading, Hiroshi was allowed to accompany her, and she took him to one side and made him promise not to let the chests out of his sight on the journey. And at the last moment she took the sword Takeo had given her.

Amano managed to persuade Hiroshi to leave his father's sword behind, but the boy brought a dagger and his bow as well as a small, fiery roan horse from his family's stables that acted up all the first day, causing the men endless amusement. Twice it wheeled round and bolted, heading for home, until the boy brought it under control and caught up with them, blue-faced with rage but otherwise undaunted.

"He's a nice-looking creature, but green," Amano said. "And you make him tense. Don't grip so hard. Relax."

He made Hiroshi ride alongside him; the horse settled down and the next day gave no problems. Kaede was happy to be on the road. As she had hoped, it kept her from brooding. The weather was fine, the country in the full flush of harvest, the men cheerful at the prospect of seeing their homes and families after months away. Hiroshi was a good companion, full of information about the land they passed through.

"I wish my father had taught me as much as yours taught you," she said, impressed by his knowledge. "When I was your age I was a hostage in Noguchi Castle."

"He made me learn all the time. He would not allow me to waste a moment."

"Life is so short and fragile," Kaede said. "Perhaps he knew he would not see you grow up."

Hiroshi nodded and rode in silence for a while.

He must miss his father, but he will not show it, she thought, and found herself envying the way he had been taught. *I will have my children brought up that way; girls as well as boys will be taught everything and will learn to be strong.*

On the morning of the third day they crossed the Shirakawa, or White River, and entered her family's domain. It was shallow and easily fordable, the swift white water swirling between rocks. There was no barrier at the border; they were beyond the jurisdiction of the great clans and in the region of smaller landholders, where neighbors either were involved in petty standoffs or had formed amicable alliances among themselves. Nominally these warrior families paid allegiance to Kumamoto or Maruyama, but they did not move to the castle towns, preferring to live on and farm their own lands, on which they paid very little tax to anyone.

"I've never crossed the Shirakawa before," Hiroshi said as the horses splashed through. "This is the farthest I've been from Maruyama."

"So now it's my turn to instruct you," she said, taking

pleasure in pointing out the landmarks of her country. "I will take you to the source of the river later, to the great caves, only you will have to wait outside."

"Why?" he demanded.

"It's a sacred place for women. No men are allowed to set foot in there."

She was eager to get home now and they did not linger on the way, but she was studying everything: the look of the land, the progress of the harvest, the condition of oxen and children. Compared to a year ago when she had returned with Shizuka, things had improved, but there were still many signs of poverty and neglect.

I abandoned them, she thought guiltily. *I should have come home before.* She thought of her tempestuous flight to Terayama in the spring: She seemed to have been another person, bewitched.

Amano had sent two of the men ahead, and Shoji Kiyoshi, the domain's senior retainer, was waiting for her at the gate of her house. He greeted her with surprise and, she thought, coolness. The household women were lined up in the garden, but there was no sign of her sisters or Ayame.

Raku whinnied, turning his head toward the stables and

the water meadows where he had run in the winter. Amano came forward to help her dismount. Hiroshi slid from the roan's back and it tried to kick the horse next to it.

"Where are my sisters?" Kaede demanded, brushing aside the women's murmured greetings.

No one answered. A shrike was calling insistently from the camphor tree by the gate, grating on her nerves.

"Lady Shirakawa . . ." Shoji began.

She spun to face him. "Where are they?"

"We were told . . . you sent instructions for them to go to Lord Fujiwara."

"I did no such thing! How long have they been there?"

"Two months at least." He glanced at the horsemen and the servants. "We should speak in private."

"Yes, at once," she agreed.

One of the women ran forward with a bowl of water.

"Welcome home, Lady Shirakawa."

Kaede washed her feet and stepped onto the veranda. Unease was beginning to creep through her. The house was eerily quiet. She wanted to hear Hana's and Ai's voices; she realized how much she had missed them.

It was a little after noon. She gave instructions for the

men to be fed, the horses watered, and both to be kept ready in case she needed them. She took Hiroshi to her own room and told him to stay there with the records while she spoke to Shoji. She was not hungry at all, but she arranged for the women to bring food to the boy. Then she went to her father's old room and sent for Shoji.

The room looked as if someone had just walked out of it. There was a brush lying on the writing table. Hana must have gone on with her studies even after Kaede's departure. She picked up the brush and was staring at it dully when Shoji tapped on the door.

He entered and knelt before her, apologizing. "We had no idea it was not your wish. It seemed so likely. Lord Fujiwara himself came and spoke to Ai."

She thought she detected insincerity in his voice. "Why did he invite them? What did he want with them?" Her voice was trembling.

"You yourself often went there," Shoji replied.

"Everything has changed since then!" she exclaimed. "Lord Otori Takeo and I were married at Terayama. We have established ourselves at Maruyama. You must have heard of this."

"I found it hard to believe," he replied, "since everyone

thought you were betrothed to Lord Fujiwara and were to marry him."

"There was no betrothal!" she said in fury. "How dare you question my marriage!"

She saw the muscles round his jaw tense and realized he was as angry as she was. He leaned forward. "What are we to think?" he hissed. "We hear of a marriage that is undertaken with no betrothal, no permission asked or given, none of your family present. I am glad your father is already dead. You killed him by the shame you brought on him, but at least he is spared this fresh shame—"

He broke off. They stared at each other, both shocked by his outburst.

I'll have to take his life, Kaede thought in horror. *He cannot speak to me like that and live. But I need him: Who else can look after things here for me?* Then the fear came to her that he might try and take the domain from her, using his anger to mask ambition and greed. She wondered if he had taken control of the men she and Kondo had gathered together in the winter—and if they would obey him now. She wished Kondo were there, then realized that she could trust the Tribe man even less than her father's senior retainer. No one could help her.

Struggling to hide her apprehension, she continued to stare at Shoji until he lowered his eyes.

He regained control of himself, wiping the spittle from his mouth. "Forgive me. I have known you since you were born. It is my duty to speak to you, even though it pains me."

"I will forgive you this time," she said. "But it is you who shame my father, through disrespect to his heir. If you ever speak to me in that fashion again, I will order you to slit your belly."

"You are only a woman," he said, trying to placate her but enraging her further. "You have no one to guide you."

"I have my husband," she said shortly. "There is nothing you or Lord Fujiwara can do to alter that. Go to him now and say my sisters are to come home at once. They will return with me to Maruyama."

He left immediately. Shocked and restless, she could not sit quietly and wait for his return. She called to Hiroshi and showed him the house and garden while she checked all the repairs that she had had done in the autumn. The crested ibis in their summer plumage were feeding on the banks of the rice fields, and the shrike continued to scold them as they trespassed into its territory. Then she told him to fetch the chests of records and, carrying one each, they made their way upstream along the Shirakawa to where it emerged from under the mountain. She would not hide them where Shoji might find them; she would entrust them to no human. She had decided to give them to the goddess.

The holy place calmed her, as always, but its ageless, sacred atmosphere awed her rather than lifted her spirits. Below the huge arch of the cave's entrance the river flowed slowly and steadily in deep pools of green water, belying its name, and the twisted shapes of the calcified rocks gleamed like mother-of-pearl in the half-light.

The old couple who maintained the shrine came out to greet her. Leaving Hiroshi in the company of the man, Kaede went forward with his wife, each of them carrying one of the chests.

Lamps and candles had been lit inside the cavern, and the damp rock glistened. The roar of the river drowned out all other noise. They stepped carefully from stone to stone, past the giant mushroom, past the frozen waterfall, past Heaven's Stairway—all shapes made by the limy water—until they came to the rock shaped like the goddess, from which drops fell like tears of mother's milk.

Kaede said, "I must ask the goddess to protect these treasures for me. Unless I myself come for them, they must stay here with her forever."

The old woman nodded and bowed. Behind the rock a cave had been hollowed out, well above the highest level of the river. They climbed up to it and placed the chests in it. Kaede noticed that it contained many other objects that had been given to the goddess. She wondered about their history and what had happened to the women who had placed them there. There was a damp, ancient smell. Some of the objects were decaying; some had already rotted. Would the records of the Tribe rot away there, hidden under the mountain?

The air was cold and clammy, making her shiver. When she put the chest down, her arms felt suddenly empty and light. She was seized by the knowledge that the goddess knew her need—that her empty arms, her empty womb, would be filled.

She knelt before the rock and scooped up water from the pool that had gathered at its base. As she drank she prayed almost wordlessly. The water was as soft as milk.

The old woman, kneeling behind her, began to chant a prayer so ancient that Kaede did not recognize the words, but its meaning washed over her and mingled with her own longing. The rock shape had no eyes, no features, yet she felt the benign gaze of the goddess upon her. She remembered the vision she had had at Terayama and the words that had been spoken to her: *Be patient; he will come for you.*

She heard the words clearly again, and for a moment they puzzled her. Then she understood them to mean he would come back. *Of course he will. I will be patient,* she vowed again. *As soon as my sisters are here, we will go to Maruyama at once. And when Takeo returns, I will conceive a child. I was right to come here.*

She felt so strengthened by the visit to the caves that at the end of the afternoon she went to the family temple to pay her respects to her father's tomb. Hiroshi came with her, as did one of the women of the house, Ayako, who carried offerings of fruit and rice and a bowl of smoking incense.

His ashes lay buried among the graves of her ancestors, the Shirakawa lords. Beneath the huge cedars it was gloomy and cool. The wind soughed in the branches, carrying the *min-min* of cicadas. Over the years earthquakes had shifted the columns and pillars, and the ground heaved upward as if the dead were trying to escape.

Her father's grave was still intact. Kaede took the offerings from Ayako and placed them in front of the stone. She clapped her hands and bowed her head. She dreaded hearing or seeing his spirit; yet she wanted to placate it. She could not think calmly about his death. He had wanted to die but had been unable to find the courage to kill himself. Shizuka and Kondo had killed him: Did that constitute murder? She was aware, too, of the part she had played, the shame she had brought on him; would his spirit now demand some payment?

She took the bowl of smoldering incense from Ayako and let the smoke waft over the tomb and over her own face and hands to purify her. She put the bowl down and clapped again three times. The wind dropped, the crickets fell silent, and in that moment she felt the earth tremble slightly beneath her. The landscape quivered. The trees shook.

"An earthquake!" Hiroshi exclaimed behind her as Ayako gave a cry of fear.

It was only a small tremor, and no more followed, but Ayako was nervous and jittery on the way home.

"Your father's spirit spoke to you," she murmured to Kaede. "What did he say?"

"He approves of everything I have done," she replied with a confidence she was far from feeling. In fact the tremor had shocked her. She feared her father's angry, embittered ghost and felt it attacked all she had experienced in the sacred caves at the goddess's feet.

"May heaven be praised," Ayako said, but her lips tightened and she continued to give Kaede anxious glances all evening.

"By the way," Kaede asked her as they ate together, "where is the young man Sunoda, Akita's nephew?" This young man had come with his uncle the previous winter, and she had made him remain in her household as a hostage, in Shoji's care. She was beginning to think she might have need of him now.

"He was allowed to return to Inuyama," Ayako said.

"What?" Shoji had relinquished her hostage? She could not believe the extent of his treachery.

"His father was said to be ill," Ayako explained.

So her hostage was gone, diminishing her power further.

It was already dusk before she heard Shoji's voice outside. Hiroshi had gone with Amano to his house to meet his family and sleep there, and Kaede had been waiting in her father's room, going through the records of the estate. She could see many signs of mismanagement, and when it was obvious Shoji had returned alone, her rage against her father's senior retainer grew even more fierce.

When he came to her Ayako followed him, bringing tea, but Kaede was too impatient to drink it.

"Where are my sisters?" she demanded.

He drank the tea gratefully before replying. He looked hot and tired. "Lord Fujiwara is glad of your return," he said. "He sends you his greetings and asks that you will call on him tomorrow. He will send his palanquin and an escort."

"I have no intention of calling on him," she retorted, trying not to lose her temper. "I expect my sisters to be returned to me tomorrow, and after that we will leave for Maruyama as soon as possible."

"I am afraid your sisters are not there," he said.

Her heart plunged to her belly. "Where are they?"

"Lord Fujiwara says Lady Shirakawa is not to be alarmed. They are perfectly safe and he will tell her where they are when she visits him tomorrow."

"You dare to bring me such a message?" Her voice sounded thin and unconvincing to her own ears.

Shoji inclined his head. "It gives me no pleasure. But Lord Fujiwara is who he is; I cannot defy or disobey him, nor, I believe, can you."

"They are hostages, then?" she said in a low voice.

He did not answer directly but merely said, "I'll give orders for your journey tomorrow. Shall I accompany you?"

"No!" she cried. "And if I am to go, I will ride. I will not wait for his palanquin. Tell Amano I will ride my gray and he is to come with me."

For a moment she thought he would argue with her, but then he bowed deeply and acquiesced.

After he had gone, her thoughts were in turmoil. If she could not trust Shoji, whom of the domain's men could she trust? Were they trying to trap her? Surely even Fujiwara would not dare. She was married now. At one moment she thought she should return immediately to Maruyama; the next she realized Ai and Hana were in someone else's possession and she understood what it meant to have hostages held against her.

So must my mother and Lady Naomi have suffered, she thought. *I must go to Fujiwara and bargain with him for them. He has helped me before. He will not turn completely against me now.*

Next she began to worry about what to do with Hiroshi. It had seemed like the safest of journeys; yet she could not help feeling that she had brought him into danger. Should he ride with her to Lord Fujiwara's or should she send him home as quickly as possible?

She rose early and sent for Amano. She dressed in the simple traveling clothes she had worn on the journey, even though she could hear Shizuka's voice in her head: *You can't appear before Lord Fujiwara on horseback like a warrior.* Her own better judgment told her to delay a few days, to send messages and gifts and then to travel in his palanquin with his escort, dressed perfectly for him, presented like the flawless treasures he prized. Shizuka, even Manami, would have advised her so. But her impatience was too great. She knew she would never endure the waiting and the inactivity. She would meet Lord Fujiwara once more, would find out where her sisters were and what he wanted, and would then go immediately back to Maruyama, back to Takeo.

When Amano came she sent the women away so she could speak privately with him, and quickly explained the situation.

"I have to go to Lord Fujiwara's, but to tell you the truth I am anxious about his intentions. We may need to leave quickly and return to Maruyama at speed. Be ready for it, and make sure the men and horses are prepared."

His eyes narrowed. "There will be no fighting, surely?"

"I don't know. I am afraid they will try to detain me."

"Against your will? It's impossible!"

"It's unlikely, I know, but I am uneasy. Why were my sisters taken away if not to force me in some way?"

"We should leave at once," he said, young enough not to be cowed by the nobleman's rank. "Let your husband talk to Lord Fujiwara with the sword."

"I am afraid of what will be done to my sisters. I must at least find out where they are. Shoji says we cannot defy Fujiwara, and I suppose he is right. I will have to go and speak with him. But I will not go into the house. Do not let them take me inside."

Amano bowed. Kaede went on: "Should Hiroshi be sent home? I wish I had not brought him; I have the burden of his safety on me now too."

"There is safety in numbers," Amano said. "He should stay with us. And anyway, if there is to be trouble, we can ill spare the men to escort him back. I will die before any harm comes to him or you."

She smiled, grateful for his loyalty. "Then let us leave with no more delay."

The weather had changed again. The clarity and coolness of the last few days had given way to a renewed oppressiveness. It was humid and still, the sort of day that heralded the typhoons of late summer. The horses were sweating and rest-less, Hiroshi's roan more unsettled than ever.

Kaede wanted to talk to Hiroshi, to warn him of the possible dangers that lay ahead, to make him promise not to get involved in any fighting; but the horse was too fidgety, and Amano made the boy ride in front with him, lest the roan upset Raku as well. She could feel the sweat running down inside her clothes. She hoped she would not arrive red in the face and soaked. She was already half regretting the rashness of her decision. But, as always, riding made her feel more powerful. She had made the journey only in the palan-quin before, never able to look out on the landscape from behind the silk curtains and oiled paper screens that had enclosed her. Now she was able to absorb the beauty of the scenery, the richness of farmland and forest, the grandeur of the distant mountains, range after range, each slightly paler than the one in front, fading until they merged into the sky.

No wonder Lord Fujiwara did not want to leave this beautiful place. His image, seductive and intriguing, rose before her eyes. She remembered how he had always seemed to like and admire her. She could not believe he would harm her. But her senses were heightened with some apprehension.

Is this how it feels to ride into battle, she wondered, *life never seeming more beautiful nor more fleeting, to be grasped and flung away in one and the same breath?*

She put her hand on the sword in her belt, reassured by the feel of the hilt.

They were only a few miles from the gates of Fujiwara's residence when they saw dust on the road ahead, and out of the haze trotted the palanquin bearers and horsemen sent by the nobleman to fetch her. Their leader spotted the silver river crest on Amano's surcoat and drew rein to greet him. His gaze swept over Kaede and then his neck muscles corded as his eyes snapped back to her in astonishment.

"Lady Shirakawa," he gasped, and shouted to the bearers, "Down! Down!"

They dropped the palanquin and knelt in the dust. The horsemen dismounted and stood with bowed heads. They appeared submissive, but she saw immediately that they outnumbered her men two to one.

"I am on my way to visit His Lordship," she said. She recognized the retainer but could not recall his name. He was the man who had always come to escort her to Lord Fujiwara's in the past.

"I am Murita," he said. "Would Lady Shirakawa not prefer to be carried?"

"I will ride," she said shortly. "We are so close now."

His lips were compressed into a thin line. *He disapproves,* she thought, and glanced at Amano and Hiroshi, who were now alongside her. Amano's face gave nothing away, but there was a flush of blood beneath Hiroshi's skin.

Are they embarrassed for me? Am I shaming myself and them? Kaede straightened her back and urged Raku forward.

Murita sent two of his men ahead, increasing her sense of unease about the reception that awaited them, but she could think of nothing to do but ride onward.

The horses felt her anxiety. Raku sidestepped a little, ears pricked, eyes rolling, and Hiroshi's horse threw its head in the air and tried to buck. The boy's knuckles were white on the reins as he brought it under control.

When they came to the residence, the gates were open and armed guards stood inside the courtyard. Amano dismounted and came to help Kaede from Raku's back.

"I will not get down until Lord Fujiwara comes," she said boldly. "I do not intend to stay."

Murita hesitated, unwilling to take such a message.

"Tell him I am here," she pressed.

"Lady Shirakawa." He bowed his head and dismounted, but at that moment Lord Fujiwara's young companion Mamoru the actor came from the house and knelt in front of her horse.

"Welcome, lady," he said. "Please come inside."

She was afraid that if she did she would never come out. "Mamoru," she said curtly, "I will not go inside. I have come to find out where my sisters are."

He stood then and came to the right side of her horse, stepping between her and Amano. He, who had rarely looked directly at her, now seemed to be trying to meet her gaze.

"Lady Shirakawa . . ." he began, and she heard something in his voice.

"Remount," she said to Amano, and he obeyed her instantly.

"Please," Mamoru said quietly, "it's best if you comply. I beg you. For your sake, for the sake of your men, the boy . . ."

"If Lord Fujiwara will not come to speak to me and will not tell me what I want to know, I have no further business here."

She did not see who gave the order. She was aware only

of some look that flashed between Mamoru and Murita.

"Ride!" she cried to Amano, and tried to turn Raku's head, but Murita was holding the bridle. She leaned forward, drawing her sword and urging the horse to rear. He shook his head free from the man's grip and went up on his hind legs, striking out with his forefeet. She struck downward at Murita and saw the blade slice against his hand. He cried out in fury, pulling out his own sword. She thought he would kill her, but he grabbed at the bridle again, wrenching the horse's head down. She felt something plunge and flail behind her: It was Hiroshi's horse, panicking. Mamoru was plucking at her clothes, calling out to her, begging her to surrender. Beyond him she could see Amano. His sword was drawn, but before he could use it an arrow struck him in the chest. She saw the look of shock come into his eyes, then blood began to bubble with each breath and he fell forward.

"No!" she screamed. Murita, at the same moment, in frustrated rage, thrust his sword upward into Raku's exposed chest. The horse screamed, too, in pain and fear, and his bright blood began to gush. As he faltered, legs swaying, head sinking, Murita caught Kaede and tried to drag her from his back. She struck out at him once more, but the horse was falling, taking her down, and her blow had no strength in it. Murita caught her wrist and effortlessly twisted the sword from her hand. Saying nothing, he half dragged, half carried her to the house.

"Help me! Help me!" she called, twisting her head round, trying to look back at her men, but the swift, ferocious assault had left them all dead or dying. "Hiroshi!" she screamed, and heard hooves pounding. The last thing she saw before Murita carried her inside was the roan bolting, carrying the boy away against his will. It was the slightest grain of comfort.

Murita searched her for other weapons, finding her knife; his hand was bleeding freely and rage made him rough. Mamoru ran before them, opening doors as he took her to the guest rooms. When he released her she fell to the ground, sobbing with rage and grief.

"Raku! Raku!" she wept, as grief-stricken as if the horse had been her child. Then she wept for Amano and the others whom she had led to their deaths.

Mamoru knelt beside her, babbling, "I'm sorry, Lady Shirakawa. You must submit. No one is going to hurt you.

Believe me, we all love and honor you here. Please calm yourself."

When she only wept more desperately, he said to the maids, "Send for Dr. Ishida."

A few minutes later she was aware of the physician's presence. He knelt beside her and she raised her head, pushing aside her hair and gazing at him with stricken eyes.

"Lady Shirakawa—" he began, but she interrupted him.

"My name is Otori. I am married. What is this outrage? You will not let them keep me here. You will tell them to let me go at once."

"I wish I could," he said in a low voice. "But we all lead our lives here according to His Lordship's will, not our own."

"What does he want from me? Why has he done this? He has abducted my sisters, murdered my men!" The tears poured anew down her face. "He did not need to kill my horse." She was racked by sobs.

Ishida told the maids to fetch herbs from his house and bring hot water. Then he examined her gently, looking in her eyes and feeling her pulse.

"Forgive me," he said, "but I must ask you if you are carrying a child."

"Why must you know that? It is nothing to do with you!"

"His Lordship's intention is to marry you. He considers that you were betrothed to him. He had already sought the emperor's permission, as well as Lord Arai's."

"We were never betrothed," Kaede sobbed. "I am married to Otori Takeo."

Ishida said gently, "I can't discuss these things with you. You will see His Lordship directly. But as your physician I must know if you are pregnant."

"What if I am?"

"Then we will get rid of it."

When Kaede cried out in grief, he said, "Lord Fujiwara is already making great concessions to you. He could have you put to death for your infidelity. He will forgive you and marry you, but he will not give his name to another man's child."

She made no response other than renewed sobbing. The maid returned with the herbs and teakettle and Ishida brewed the infusion.

"Drink it," he told Kaede. "It will calm you."

"Suppose I refuse?" she said, sitting abruptly and snatching the bowl from him. She held it out at arm's length as though she would pour it onto the matting. "Suppose I refuse all food and drink? Will he marry a corpse?"

"Then you condemn your sisters to death—or worse," he said. "I'm sorry, I take no pleasure in the situation, nor am I proud of my part in it. All I can do is be utterly truthful with you. If you submit to His Lordship's will, you will preserve your honor and their lives."

She gazed at him for a long moment. Slowly she brought the cup to her lips. "I am not pregnant," she said, and drained it.

Ishida sat with her while her senses began to numb, and when she was calm, he told the maids to take her to the bath-house and wash the blood from her.

By the time she was bathed and dressed, the infusion had dulled her grief and the brief murderous episode seemed like something she had dreamed. In the afternoon she even slept a little, hearing as if from another country the chanting of the priests lifting the pollution of death from the house and restoring it to its peace and harmony. When she woke and found herself in the familiar room, she forgot for a moment the past months and thought, *I am at Fujiwara's. How long have I stayed here? I must call Shizuka and ask her.*

Then she remembered but with no intensity, just a dull knowledge of what had been snatched so violently from her.

It was twilight, the cool ending to a long, heavy day. She could hear the soft footsteps of the servants and their whispered voices. A maid came to the room with a tray of food. Kaede picked at it listlessly; the smell of food sickened her and she soon called for it to be taken away.

The maid returned with tea. She was followed into the room by another woman, middle-aged, with small sharp eyes and a severe look, obviously not a servant from her elegant clothes and refined manner. She bowed to the ground before Kaede and said, "I am Ono Rieko, a cousin of Lord Fujiwara's late wife. I spent many years in Her Ladyship's household. His Lordship sent for me to make the preparations for the wedding ceremony. Please accept me with kindness." She bowed her head formally to the floor again.

Kaede felt an instinctive dislike for the woman before her. Her appearance was not unpleasing—she could not imagine Fujiwara suffering any person around him who was not attractive—but she sensed both self-pride and mean-spiritedness in her character.

"Do I have any choice?" she said coldly.

Rieko gave a little trill of laughter as she sat up. "I am sure Lady Shirakawa will change her mind about me. I am only a very ordinary person, but there may be things I can advise you on." She began to pour the tea, saying, "Dr. Ishida wants you to have a cup of this now. And as it is the first night of the moon, Lord Fujiwara will come shortly to welcome you, and view the new moon with you. Drink your tea and I'll make sure your hair and dress are appropriate."

Kaede took a sip of tea and then another, trying not to gulp it down, for she was terribly thirsty. She was calm and could barely feel anything; yet she was aware of the slow thudding of blood behind her temples. She dreaded meeting him, dreaded the power he had over her. It was the power that men held over women everywhere, in every aspect of their lives. She must have been mad to think she could fight it. She remembered all too clearly Lady Naomi's words: *I must appear a defenseless woman, otherwise these warriors will crush me.*

Now they were crushing her. Shizuka had warned her that her marriage would enrage the elders of her class—that it would never be permitted. But if she had listened and done what she was told, she would never have had the months with Takeo. The thought of him now was so freshly painful, even with the calming tea, that she laid it away in the secret recesses of her heart, as hidden as the records of the Tribe in the Sacred Caves.

She became aware that Rieko was studying her closely. She turned her face away and took another sip of tea.

"Come, come, Lady Shirakawa," Rieko said briskly. "You must not brood. You are about to make a brilliant marriage." She came a little closer, shuffling forward on her knees. "You are as beautiful as they say, apart from being too tall, but your skin has a tendency to sallowness, and that heavy look does not become you. Your beauty is your greatest asset: We must do all we can to preserve it."

She took the cup and set it on the tray. Then she unloosened Kaede's hair from the ties that held it back and began to comb it out.

"How old are you?"

"Sixteen," Kaede replied.

"I thought you were older, twenty at least. You must be the type that ages rapidly. We'll have to watch that." The comb raked across Kaede's scalp, bringing tears of pain to her eyes.

Rieko said, "It must be very difficult to dress your hair; it is very soft."

"I usually tie it back," Kaede said.

"It is the fashion in the capital to wear it piled on the head," Rieko said, tugging in a way that hurt intentionally. "Thicker, coarser hair is more desirable."

Whereas sympathy and understanding might have released Kaede's grief, Rieko's unkindness steeled her, making her determined never to break down, never to show her feelings. *I slept in ice,* she thought. *The goddess speaks to me. I will discover power of some sort here and use it until Takeo comes for me.* He would come, she knew, or die in the attempt, and when she saw his lifeless corpse she would be freed from her promise and she would join him in the shadows of the afterworld.

In the distance dogs began barking suddenly and excitedly, and a moment later the house shook in a tremor, longer and a little more severe than the previous day's.

Kaede felt what she always felt: shock, amazement that the earth could quiver like fresh bean curd, and a sort of elation that nothing was fixed or certain. Nothing lasted forever, not even Fujiwara and his house full of treasures.

Rieko dropped the comb and struggled to her feet. The maids came running to the door.

"Come outside quickly," Rieko cried, her voice alarmed.

"Why?" Kaede said. "The quake will not be a big one."

Rieko had already left the room. Kaede could hear her ordering the maids to extinguish all the lamps, almost shrieking at them in her panic. Kaede remained where she was, listening to the running feet, the raised voices, the barking dogs. After a few moments she took up the comb and finished combing out her hair. Since her head ached, she left it loose.

The robe they had dressed her in earlier seemed quite suitable for moon viewing: It was dove gray, embroidered with bush clover and pale lemon warblers. She wanted to look at the moon, to be bathed in its silvery light, and to be reminded of how it came and went in the heavens, disappeared for three days, and then returned.

The maids had left the doors to the veranda open. Kaede stepped out and knelt on the wooden floor, gazing toward the mountain, recalling how she had sat here with Fujiwara, wrapped in bearskins as the snow fell.

Another slight tremor came, but she felt no fear. She saw the mountain tremble against the pale violet sky. The dark shapes of the garden trees were swaying, though there was no wind, and birds, disturbed, were calling as if it were dawn.

Slowly their calls subsided and the dogs fell quiet. The thin golden sickle of the new moon hung next to the evening star just above the peaks. Kaede closed her eyes.

She smelled Fujiwara's fragrance before she heard him. Then she caught the tread of feet, the rustle of silk. She opened her eyes.

He stood a few feet away from her, staring at her with the rapt, covetous look that she remembered so well.

"Lady Shirakawa."

"Lord Fujiwara." She returned his gaze for longer than she should before slowly prostrating herself until her brow touched the floor.

Fujiwara stepped onto the veranda, followed by Mamoru, who was carrying carpets and cushions. Not until the nobleman was seated did he give Kaede permission to sit up. He reached out and touched the silk robe.

"It's very becoming. I thought it would be. You gave poor Murita quite a shock when you turned up on horseback. He nearly speared you by mistake."

She thought she would faint from the fury that suddenly erupted through the herb-induced tranquillity. That he should allude so lightly, jokingly, to the murders of her men, of Amano, who had known her since she was a child . . .

"How dare you do this to me?" she said, and heard Mamoru's gasp of shock. "I was married three months ago to Otori Takeo at Terayama. My husband will punish you—" She broke off, trying to regain control.

"I thought we would enjoy the moon before we talked," he replied, showing no response to the insulting way she had spoken. "Where are your women? Why are you here alone?"

"They ran when the earth shook," she replied shortly.

"Were you not afraid?"

"I have nothing to be afraid of. You have already done the worst anyone can do to me."

"It seems we are to talk now," he said. "Mamoru, bring wine and then see that we are undisturbed."

He looked meditatively at the moon without speaking for the next few minutes until Mamoru came back. When the young man had retired into the shadows again, Fujiwara indicated that Kaede should pour the wine. He drank and said, "Your marriage to the person who calls himself Otori Takeo has been set aside. It was undertaken without permission and has been ruled invalid."

"By whose authority?"

"Lord Arai; your own senior retainer, Shoji; and myself. The Otori have already disowned Takeo and declared his adoption illegal. The general opinion was that you should die for your disobedience to Arai and your infidelity to me, especially when your involvement in Iida's death became more widely known."

"We had an agreement that you would share my secrets with no one," she said.

"I thought we had an agreement that we would marry."

She could make no response without insulting him further, and his words had in fact frightened her. She was all too aware that he could order her death on a moment's whim. No one would dare either to disobey such an order or to judge him afterward.

He went on: "You are aware of my high regard for you. I was able to effect something of a transaction with Arai. He agreed to spare you if I married you and kept you in seclusion. I will support his cause with the emperor in due course. In return I sent your sisters to him."

"You gave them to Arai? They are in Inuyama?"

"I believe it's quite common to hand women over as

hostages," he returned. "Arai was incensed, by the way, when you dared to keep Akita's nephew as your hostage. It could have been a good move, but you threw all that away when you acted so rashly in the spring. All it achieved, then, was to offend Arai and his retainers further. Arai was your champion before. It was very foolhardy to treat him so badly."

"I know now that Shoji betrayed me," she said bitterly. "Akita's nephew should never have been allowed to go home."

"You mustn't be harsh on Shoji." Fujiwara's voice was bland and calm. "He was doing what he thought right for you and your family. As are we all. I would like our marriage to take place as soon as possible: I think before the end of the week. Rieko will instruct you in your dress and behavior."

She felt despair descend on her like the hunter's net over the wild duck. "All men involved with me have died except my lawful husband, Lord Otori Takeo. Aren't you afraid?"

"Common talk is that it is men who desire you who die; I feel no more desire for you than I ever did. I do not want more children. Our marriage is to save your life. It will be in name only." He drank again and placed the cup on the floor. "It would be appropriate now to express your gratitude."

"I am to be just one of your possessions?"

"Lady Shirakawa, you are one of the few people I have shared my treasures with—the only woman. You know how I like to keep them away from the eyes of the world, wrapped up, hidden."

Her heart quailed. She said nothing.

"And don't think Takeo will come and rescue you. Arai is determined to punish him. He is mounting a campaign against him now. The domains of Maruyama and Shirakawa will be taken in your name and given to me as your husband." He let his gaze cover her as if he would drink in every drop of her suffering. "His desire for you has indeed been his downfall. Takeo will be dead before winter."

Kaede had studied Fujiwara throughout the previous winter and knew all the changing expressions of his face. He liked to think he was impassive, his feelings always perfectly controlled, but she had grown adept at reading him. She heard the note of cruelty in his voice, and caught the taste of pleasure on his tongue. She had heard it before when he spoke Takeo's name. She had thought him almost infatuated with Takeo when she had told him her secrets when the snow lay thick on the ground and icicles as long as men's legs hung from the eaves. She had seen the gleam of desire in his eye, the slight slackening of his mouth, the way his tongue swelled around the name. Now she realized that the nobleman desired Takeo's death. It would give him pleasure and set him free from his obsession. And she had no doubt that her suffering would heighten his pleasure.

At that moment she resolved two things: She would show him nothing, and she would live. She would submit to his will so that he had no excuse to kill her before Takeo came for her, but she would never give either him or the devil woman he'd assigned to her the satisfaction of seeing how deeply she suffered.

She allowed her eyes to fill with contempt as she looked at Fujiwara, and then she gazed past him at the moon.

The marriage took place a few days later. Kaede drank the infusions Ishida brewed, thankful for the numbness they brought her. She was resolved to have no feelings, to be like ice, remembering how long ago it was that Takeo's gaze had plunged her into the deep, cold sleep. She did not blame Ishida or Mamoru for the part they played in her imprisonment, for she knew they were bound by the same rigid code she was, but she swore Murita would pay for the murder of her men and her horse, and she came to loathe Rieko.

She watched herself go through the rituals as if she were a doll or a puppet manipulated on a stage. Her family were represented by Shoji and two of her retainers; one she knew was a brother of Hirogawa, the man she had had executed by Kondo when he had refused to serve her the day of her father's death. *I should have taken the lives of his whole family,* she thought bitterly. *I spared them only to make an enemy of them.* There were other men there, of high rank, who she imagined must have been sent by Arai. They did not acknowledge her in any way and she was not told their names. It made her realize all too clearly her new position: no longer mistress of a domain, her husband's ally and equal, but second wife to a nobleman, with no other life than what he saw fit to allow her.

It was an elaborate ceremony, far more lavish than her wedding at Terayama. The prayers and chanting seemed to go on endlessly. The incense and bells made her head swim, and when she had to exchange the ritual three cups of wine three times with her new husband, she feared she would faint. She had eaten so little all week, she felt like a wraith.

The day was unnaturally oppressive and still. Toward evening it began to rain heavily.

She was taken from the shrine by palanquin, and Rieko and the other women undressed and bathed her. They rubbed creams into her skin and perfumed her hair. She was clad in night robes, more sumptuous than those she usually wore in the day. Then she was taken to new apartments, in the deep interior of the residence, ones she had never seen before nor even known existed. They had been newly decorated. The beams and bosses glowed with gold leaf, the screens had been painted with birds and flowers, and the straw matting was fresh and sweet-smelling. The heavy rain made the rooms dim, but dozens of lamps burned in ornately carved metal stands.

"All this is for you," Rieko said, a note of envy in her voice.

Kaede did not reply. She wanted to say, *For what purpose, seeing that he will never lie with me?*—but what business was this of Rieko's? Then the thought came to her: Maybe he intended to, just once, as he had with his first wife to conceive his son. She began to tremble with revulsion and fear.

"You don't need to be afraid," Rieko sneered. "It's not as if you don't know what to expect from marriage. Now, if you were, as you should be, a virgin . . ."

Kaede could not believe that the woman dared to speak to her in such a manner and in front of the servants.

"Tell the maids to leave us," she said, and when they were alone: "If you insult me again I shall see that you are dismissed."

Rieko laughed her empty trilling laugh. "I don't think my lady quite understands her situation. Lord Fujiwara will never dismiss me. If I were you, I would be more afraid for my own future. If you transgress in any way—if your behavior is anything less than what is expected of Lord Fujiwara's wife—*you* may find *yourself* dismissed. You think you are brave and that you would have the courage to take your own life. Let me tell you, it is harder than it seems. When it comes to the point, most women fail. We cling to life, weak things that we are." She picked up a lamp and raised it so the light fell on Kaede's face. "You have probably been told all your life that you are beautiful, but you are less beautiful now than you were a week ago, and in a year you will be less beautiful still. You have reached your peak; from now on your beauty will fade."

She held the lamp a little closer. Kaede could feel the scorch of the flame on her cheek.

"I could scar you now," Rieko hissed. "You would be turned out of the house. Lord Fujiwara will only keep you while you please his eye. After that, the only place for women like you is the brothel."

Kaede stared back without flinching. The flame flickered between them. Outside the wind was rising and a sudden gust shook the building. Far in the distance, as if from another country, a dog was howling.

Rieko laughed again and placed the lamp on the floor. "So it is not for Your Ladyship to speak of dismissing me. But I expect you are overwrought. I will forgive you. We must be good friends as His Lordship desires. He will come to you soon. I will be in the next room."

Kaede sat perfectly still listening to the rising wind. She could not help thinking about her wedding night with Takeo, the feel of his skin against hers, his lips against the back of her neck when he lifted away the weight of her hair, the pleasure he brought to her whole body before he entered her and they became one person. She tried to keep the memories at bay, but desire had taken hold of her and it threatened to melt her icy numbness.

She heard footsteps outside and held herself rigid. She

had vowed not to give her feelings away, but she was sure her aching body would somehow betray her.

Leaving his servants outside, Fujiwara stepped into the room. Kaede immediately bowed to the ground before him, not wanting him to see her face, but the act of submission itself made her tremble more.

Mamoru came in behind the nobleman, carrying a small carved chest made of paulownia wood. He placed it on the ground, bowed deeply, and crawled backward to the door of the adjoining room.

"Sit up, my dear wife," Lord Fujiwara said, and as she did so she saw Rieko pass a wine flask through the door to Mamoru. The woman bowed and crept out of sight but not, Kaede knew, out of earshot.

Mamoru poured wine and Fujiwara drank, gazing at Kaede with rapt attention. The young man passed a cup to her and she raised it to her lips. The taste was sweet and strong. She took only the smallest sip. It seemed that everything conspired to set her body on fire.

"I don't believe she has ever looked so lovely," Lord Fujiwara remarked to Mamoru. "Note how suffering has brought out the perfect shape of her face. The eyes have a deeper expression and the mouth is molded like a woman's now. It will be a challenge to capture that."

Mamoru bowed without replying.

After a short silence Fujiwara said, "Leave us alone," and when the young man had gone, he picked up the chest and rose to his feet.

"Come," he said to Kaede.

She followed him like a sleepwalker. Some unseen servant slid open the screen at the rear of the room and they stepped into another chamber. Here beds had been spread out with silk-covered quilts and wooden pillow blocks. The room was scented with a heavy fragrance. The screens closed and they were alone together.

"There is no need to be unduly alarmed," Fujiwara said. "Or perhaps I have misjudged you and it will be disappointment you feel."

She felt for the first time the sting of his contempt. He had read her clearly, had discerned her desire. A wave of heat swept over her.

"Sit down," he said.

She sank to the ground, keeping her eyes lowered. He also sat, placing the chest between them.

"We must pass a little time together. It's only a formality."

Kaede did not reply, not knowing what to say.

"Speak to me," he ordered. "Tell me something interesting or amusing."

It seemed a complete impossibility. Finally she said, "May I ask Lord Fujiwara a question?"

"You may."

"What am I to do here? How am I to spend my days?"

"Doing whatever it is that women do. Rieko will instruct you."

"May I continue my studies?"

"I think educating a girl was something of a mistake. It does not seem to have improved your character. You may read a little—K'ung Fu-Tzu, I suggest."

The wind gusted more strongly. Here in the center of the house they were protected from its full force, but even so, the beams and pillars shook and the roof creaked.

"May I see my sisters?"

"When Lord Arai has finished his campaign against the Otori, we may go to Inuyama in a year or so."

"May I write to them?" Kaede said, feeling fury build within her that she should have to beg for such favors.

"If you show Ono Rieko your letters."

The lamp flames flickered in the draft and the wind moaned outside in an almost human voice. Kaede thought suddenly of the maids she'd slept alongside at Noguchi Castle. On wild, stormy nights, when the wind kept everyone awake, they would scare each other more with ghost stories. Now she felt she could hear the same ghostly voices she'd imagined then in the many-tongued speech of the wind. The maids' stories were all of girls like themselves who'd been killed unjustly or had died for love, who had been abandoned by their lovers, betrayed by their husbands, murdered by their overlords. Their angry, jealous ghosts cried out for justice from the world of the shades. She shivered a little.

"You are cold?"

"No, I was thinking of ghosts. Maybe one touched me. The wind is strengthening. Is it a typhoon?"

"I believe so," he replied.

Takeo, where are you? she thought. *Are you out somewhere in this weather? Are you thinking of me at this moment? Is it your ghost that hangs behind me, making me shiver?*

Fujiwara was watching her. "One of the many things I admire about you is that you show no fear. Not in the earthquake, not in a typhoon. Most women are thrown into a panic by these things. Of course, that does seem more feminine, and your boldness has taken you too far. You must be protected from it."

He must never know how afraid I am of hearing of their deaths, she thought. *Takeo most, but also Ai and Hana. I must never show it.*

Fujiwara leaned forward slightly and, with one pale, long-fingered hand, indicated she should look at the chest.

"I have brought a wedding gift for you," he said, opening the lid and lifting out an object wrapped in silk. "I don't expect you are familiar with these curiosities. Some are of great antiquity. I have been collecting them for years."

He placed it on the floor in front of her. "You may look at it when I have left you."

Kaede eyed the package warily. His tone warned her that he was enjoying some kind of cruel teasing at her expense. She had no idea what it might be: a small statue, perhaps, or a flask of perfume.

She raised her eyes to his face and saw the slight smile play on his lips. She had no weapons and no defenses against him except her beauty and her courage. She gazed past him, serene and immobile.

He stood and wished her good night. She bowed to the floor as he left. The wind shook the roof and the rain lashed against it. She could not hear his footsteps as he walked away: It was as if he disappeared into the storm.

She was alone, though she knew Rieko and the maids were waiting in the adjoining rooms. She let her gaze fall on the deep purple silk and after a few moments picked it up and unwrapped the object inside.

It was an erect male member, carved from some reddish, silky wood, cherry perhaps, and perfect in every detail. She was both repelled and fascinated by it, as no doubt Fujiwara had known she would be. He would never touch her body, he would never sleep with her, but he had read her awakened desire, and with this perverse gift he was both despising and tormenting her.

Tears sprang into her eyes then. She rewrapped the carving and placed it back in the box. Then she lay down on the mattress in her marriage chamber and wept silently for the man she loved and desired.

· 2 ·

I feared I would have to report your disappearance to your wife," Makoto said as we made our way through the darkness to the shrine. "I dreaded it more than any battle I have ever faced."

"I was afraid you would have deserted me," I replied.

"I hope you know me better than that! It would have been my duty to tell Lady Otori, but I was going to leave Jiro here with horses and food and return as soon as I had spoken to her." He added in a low voice, "I would never desert you, Takeo; you must know that."

I felt ashamed of my doubts and did not share them with him.

He called to the men who were keeping guard and they shouted in reply.

"Are you all awake?" I said, for usually we shared the night watch and slept in turns.

"None of us felt like sleep," he replied. "The night is too still and heavy. The recent storm, the one that delayed you, came up out of nowhere. And for the last couple of days we've had the feeling there is someone spying on us. Yesterday, Jiro went to look for wild yams in the forest and saw someone lurking in the trees. I thought the bandits the fisherman mentioned might have got word of our presence and were checking out our strength."

We'd been making more noise than a team of oxen as we stumbled along the overgrown path. If anyone was spying on us, they would have no doubt of my return.

"They're probably afraid we're competition," I said. "As soon as we get back with more men we'll get rid of them, but the six of us can't take them on now. We'll leave at first light and hope they don't ambush us on the road."

It was impossible to tell what hour it was or how long it would be till dawn. The old shrine buildings were full of strange noises, creaks from the timber, rustling in the thatch.

Owls called all night from the woods, and once I heard a pad of feet: a wild dog, perhaps, or maybe even a wolf. I tried to sleep, but my mind was full of all those who wanted to kill me. It was quite possible that we had been traced here, and the delay made it even more likely. The fisherman—Ryoma, even—might have let slip something about my trip to Oshima, and I knew only too well that the Tribe's spies were everywhere. Quite apart from the edict they had issued against me, many of them would now feel bound by blood feuds to avenge their relatives.

Though by day I might believe in the truth of the prophecy, as always in the early hours of the morning I found it less comforting. I was inching toward achieving my goal; I could not bear the thought of dying before I'd succeeded. But with so many arrayed against me, was I as much of a lunatic as Jo-An to believe I could overcome them?

I must have dozed off, for when I next opened my eyes the sky was light gray and birds were starting to sing. Jiro was still asleep next to me, breathing deeply and evenly like a child. I touched his shoulder to wake him and he opened his eyes, smiling. Then as he returned from the other world I saw disappointment and grief spring into his face.

"Were you dreaming?" I said.

"Yes. I saw my brother. I was so glad he was alive after all. He called to me to follow him and then walked away into the forest behind our house." He made a visible effort to master his emotions and got to his feet. "We're leaving right away, aren't we? I'll go and get the horses ready."

I thought of the dream I had had about my mother and wondered what the dead were trying to tell us. In the dawn light the shrine looked more ghostly than ever. It was a bitter, hostile place and I could not wait to leave it.

The horses were fresh after the days of rest, and we rode fast. It was still hot and oppressive, with gray clouds and no wind. I looked back at the beach as we went up the cliff path, wondering about the fisherman and his remaining child, but there was no sign of life from the hovels. We were all jumpy. My ears were alert to every sound, straining to hear above the pounding of the horses' feet and the creak and jingle of the harness as well as the dull roaring of the sea.

At the top of the cliff I halted for a moment and gazed out toward Oshima. It was hidden in the mist, but a heavy crown of clouds showed where it lay.

Jiro had stopped alongside me, the others riding on into

the forest ahead. There was a moment of silence, and in that moment I heard the unmistakable sound, somewhere between a creak and a sigh, of a bowstring being drawn.

I shouted out a warning to Jiro and tried to reach him to push him down, but Shun leaped sideways, almost unseating me, and I found myself clinging to his neck. Jiro turned his head and looked toward the forest. The arrow passed whistling above me and struck him in the eye.

He let out a cry of shock and pain; his hands went to his face and then he fell forward onto his horse's neck. The horse neighed in alarm, bucked a little, and tried to take off after its companions in front, its rider swinging helplessly from side to side.

Shun stretched out his neck and went snaking across the ground toward the shelter of the trees. Ahead, Makoto and the guards had turned. One of the men rode forward and managed to grab the panicked horse by the bridle.

Makoto lifted Jiro from the saddle, but by the time I reached them the boy had died. The arrow had penetrated right through his head, shattering the back of the skull. I dismounted, cut off the bolt, and drew out the shaft. The arrow was massive and fletched with eagle feathers. The bow that had sent it must have been huge, the sort that solitary bowmen use.

I was filled with almost unbearable anguish. The shot had been meant for me. If I had not heard it and evaded it, Jiro would not be dead. Mad rage erupted in me. I would kill his murderer or die myself.

Makoto said in a whisper, "It must be an ambush. Let's take shelter and see how many there are."

"No, this was meant for me," I replied, as quietly. "This is the work of the Tribe. Stay here; take cover. I'm going after him. There will be only one—two at the most." I did not want the men with me. Only I could move silently and invisibly; only I had the skills to get close to this assassin. "Come when I call you; I want to take him alive."

Makoto said, "If there's only one, rather than take cover we'll ride on. Give me your helmet; I'll ride Shun. We may be able to confuse him. He'll follow us and you can come on him from behind."

I did not know how far this deception would work or how close the bowman was. He would have seen the arrow miss me. He would guess I'd be after him. But if my men rode ahead, at least they would not be hindering me. The bowman might be anywhere in the forest by now, but I reckoned I could move faster and more silently than he could. As the horses trotted off with their sad burden, I went invisible and ran up the slope, threading my way between the trees. I did not think the bowman would have stayed in the place from which he had sent the fatal arrow; I figured he would have moved in a south-west direction to cut us off where the road turned back to the south. But even if he was still watching us, unless he had supreme Tribe skills, he would not know where I was now.

Before long I heard the sounds of a man breathing and the slight pressure of a foot on the soft earth. I stopped and held my own breath. He passed within ten paces of me without seeing me.

It was Kikuta Hajime, the young wrestler from Matsue, with whom I had trained. I had last seen him at the wrestlers' stable when I had left for Hagi with Akio. I had imagined then that he had thought he would never see me again. But Akio had not been able to kill me as he had planned, and now Hajime had been sent against me. The huge bow was slung over his shoulder; he moved, like most heavy men, balanced on the outside of his feet and, despite his weight, swiftly and silently. Only my ears could have discerned him.

I followed him toward the road where I could hear the horses ahead of us, moving at a swift canter as if in flight. I even heard one of the guards shout to Makoto to ride faster, addressing him as Lord Otori, making me grin bitterly at the deception. My quarry and I went at speed up the slope and down again and came out on a rocky outcrop that gave a good vantage point over the road beneath.

Hajime planted his feet firmly on the rock and took the bow from his shoulder. He set the arrow in the cord; I heard him take a deep breath as he drew it back: The muscles stood out on his arms and rippled across his neck. In close combat with him I wouldn't stand a chance. I could probably get him with Jato if I took him from behind, but I'd have to be sure to kill him with the first blow, and I wanted to take him alive.

He stood motionless, waiting for his target to appear from under the trees. I could barely hear his breathing now. I knew the technique he was using and I was familiar enough with the training he'd undergone to recognize his total concentration. He was one with the bow, with the arrow. It was probably a magnificent sight, but all I was aware of was my desire to see him suffer and then die. I tried to calm my rage. I had only a few moments to think.

I still carried on me my Tribe weapons, among them a set of throwing knives. I was no expert with them, but they might answer my purpose now. I had dried and oiled them after my soaking in the pirates' harbor; they slipped silkily from their holster. As the horses approached below, I ran, still invisible, out from my hiding place, throwing the knives as I went.

The first two sailed past him, breaking his concentration and making him turn toward me. He was looking over my head with the same puzzled expression he'd worn in the training hall when I had used invisibility there. It made me want to laugh and pained me beyond words at one and the same time. The third knife caught him on the cheek, its many points making blood flower immediately. He took an involuntary step backward and I saw he was right on the brink. I threw the next two knives directly at his face and came back to visibility right in front of him. Jato sprang into my hand. He threw himself backward to avoid the blow and went over the edge, falling heavily almost under the horses' feet.

He was winded by the fall and bleeding from cheek and eyes, but it still took the five of us more than a brief struggle to subdue him. He did not utter a sound, but his eyes burned with rage and malevolence. I had to decide whether to kill him on the spot or drag him back to Maruyama, where I would devise a slow death for him that might assuage my grief for Jiro.

Once Hajime was trussed up and unable to move, I drew Makoto aside to ask his advice. I could not get out of my head the memory of how Hajime and I had trained together; we had almost been friends. Such was the code of the Tribe that it transcended any personal liking or loyalty. Didn't I already know that from my own experience, from Kenji's betrayal of Shigeru? Yet I was shocked by it all over again.

Hajime called to me, "Hey, dog!"

One of the guards kicked him. "How dare you address Lord Otori in that fashion."

"Come here, Lord Otori," the wrestler sneered. "I have something to tell you."

I went to him.

"The Kikuta have your son," he said. "And his mother is dead."

"Yuki is dead?"

"Once the boy was born, they made her take poison. Akio will raise him alone. The Kikuta will get you. You betrayed them; they will never let you live. And they have your son."

He made an almost animal-like snarl and, extending his tongue out to its fullest length, clamped his teeth down through it, biting it off. His eyes were wild with pain and rage; yet he did not make another sound. He spat out his tongue and a gush of blood followed it. It filled his throat, choking him. His powerful body arched and struggled, fighting the death his will imposed on it as he drowned in his own blood.

I turned away, sickened, and saddened beyond belief. My rage had abated. In its place was a leaden heaviness, as if the sky had fallen into my soul. I ordered the men to drag him into the forest, cut off his head, and leave his body for the wolves and foxes.

Jiro's body we took with us. We stopped at a small town along the coast, Ohama, where we held the burial service at the local shrine and paid for a stone lantern to be erected for him beneath the cedars. We donated the bow and arrows to the shrine, and I believe they still hang there, up under the rafters along with the votive pictures of horses, for the place was sacred to the horse goddess.

Among the pictures are my horses. We had to stay in the town for nearly two weeks, first to conduct the funeral ceremonies and cleanse ourselves from the pollution of death, and then for the Festival of the Dead. I borrowed an inkstone and brushes from the priest and painted Shun's picture on a slab of wood. Into it I believe I put not only my respect and gratitude for the horse that had saved my life again but also my grief for Jiro, for Yuki, for my life that seemed to lead me only into witnessing the deaths of others. And maybe my longing for Kaede, whom I missed with physical pain as grief set alight my desire for her.

I painted obsessively: Shun, Raku, Kyu, Aoi. It was a long time since I had painted, and the brush in my hand, the cool wash of the ink, had a calming effect on me. As I sat alone in the tranquil temple, I allowed myself to fantasize that this was my whole life. I had retired from the world and spent my days painting votive pictures for pilgrims. I recalled the words of the abbot at Terayama on my first visit there so long ago with Shigeru: *Come back when this is all over. There will be a place for you here.*

Will it ever be over? I asked, as I had then.

Often I found tears spring to my eyes. I grieved for Jiro and for Yuki, for their short lives, for their devotion to me, which I had not deserved, for their murders on my account. I longed to avenge them, but the brutality of Hajime's suicide had repelled me. What endless cycle of death and revenge had I initiated? I recalled all that Yuki and I had experienced together, and bitterly regretted . . . what? That I had not loved her? Maybe I had not loved her with the passion I felt for Kaede, but I had desired her, and the memory of it made me ache with desire all over again and weep again for her lithe body now stilled forever.

I was glad the solemnities of the Festival of the Dead gave me the chance to say farewell to her spirit. I lit candles for all the dead who had gone before me and asked them for their forgiveness and their guidance. It was a year since I had stood on the bank of the river at Yamagata with Shigeru and we had sent our little flaming boats adrift on the current; a year since I had spoken Kaede's name, seen her face come alight, and known that she loved me.

Desire tormented me. I could have lain with Makoto and so eased it, as well as comforted him in his grief, but though I was often tempted, something held me back. During the day, while I painted for hours, I meditated on the past year and all I had done in it, my mistakes and the pain and suffering they had inflicted on those around me. Apart from my decision to go with the Tribe, all my mistakes, I came to realize, sprang from uncontrolled desire. If I had not slept with Makoto, his obsession would not have led him to expose Kaede to her father. If I had not slept with her, she would not have nearly died when she lost our child. And if I had not slept with Yuki, she would still be alive and the son that would kill me would never have been born. I found myself thinking of Shigeru, who had resisted marrying and puzzled his household by his abstinence because he had vowed to Lady Maruyama that he would lie with no one but her. I knew of no other man who had made such a vow, but the more I thought about it, the more I wanted to emulate him in this as in everything I did. Kneeling silently before the horse-headed Kannon, I made a vow to the goddess that all my love, physical and emotional, from now on would be given only to Kaede, to my wife.

Our separation had made me realize anew how much I needed her, how she was the fixed point that steadied and strengthened my life. My love for her was the antidote to the poison that rage and grief had sent through me; like all antidotes I kept it well hidden and well guarded.

Makoto, as grief-stricken as I, also spent long hours in silent meditation. We hardly spoke during the day, but after the evening meal we often talked until far into the night. He, of course, had heard Hajime's words to me and tried to ask me about Yuki, about my son, but at first I could not bear to speak of either of them. However, on the first night of the festival, after we returned from the shore we drank a little wine together. Relieved that the coolness between us seemed to have vanished, and trusting him completely as I trusted no other man, I felt I should tell him the words of the prophecy.

He listened carefully as I described the ancient blind woman, her saintly appearance, the cave, the prayer wheel, and the sign of the Hidden.

"I have heard of her," he said. "Many people aspiring to holiness go to seek her, but I have never known anyone else who has found the way."

"I was taken by the outcast, Jo-An."

He was silent. It was a warm, still night, and all the screens stood open. The full moon poured its light over the shrine and the sacred grove. The sea roared on the shingle beach. A gecko crossed the ceiling, its tiny feet sucking at the beams. Mosquitoes whined and moths fluttered around the lamps. I extinguished the flames so they would not burn their wings: The moon was bright enough to light the room.

Makoto said finally, "Then I must accept that he is favored by the Enlightened One, as you are."

"The saint told me, '*It is all one,*'" I said. "I did not understand at the time, but later at Terayama I remembered Shigeru's words just before his death, and the truth of what she said was revealed to me."

"You cannot put it into words?"

"No, but it is true, and I live my life by it. There are no distinctions between us: Our castes as much as our beliefs are illusions that come between us and truth. It is how heaven deals with all men, and how I must too."

"I followed you because of my love for you and because I believe in the justice of your cause," he said, smiling. "I did not realize you were to be my spiritual adviser too!"

"I know nothing of spiritual matters," I said, suspecting he was laughing at me. "I have abandoned the beliefs of my childhood and I cannot take on any others in their place. All religious teachings seem to me to be made up half of deep truth and half of utter madness. People cling to their beliefs as if they could be saved by them, but beyond all the teachings there is a place of truth where it is all one."

Makoto laughed. "You seem to have more insight in your ignorance than I after years of study and debate. What else did the saint say to you?"

I repeated the words of the prophecy to him: *"'Three bloods are mixed in you. You were born into the Hidden, but your life has been brought into the open and is no longer your own. Earth will deliver what heaven desires. Your lands will stretch from sea to sea. Five battles will buy your peace, four to win and one to lose.'"*

I paused at that point, not certain whether to go on.

"Five battles?" Makoto said. "How many have we fought?"

"Two, if we count Jin-emon and the bandits."

"So that was why you asked if the fight could be called a battle! Do you believe it all?"

"Most of the time. Should I not?"

"I would believe anything I heard from her if I had the good fortune to kneel at her feet," Makoto said quietly. "Was there anything more?"

"'Many must die,'" I quoted, *"'but you yourself are safe from death, except at the hands of your own son.'"*

"I am sorry," he said with compassion. "That is a terrible burden for any man to bear, especially you who have such a strong bond with children. I imagine you long to have your own sons."

It touched me that he knew my character so well. "When I thought Kaede was lost to me forever, when I first went to the Tribe, I slept with the girl who helped me bring Shigeru out of Inuyama. Her name was Yuki. It was she who took his head to the temple."

"I remember her," Makoto said quietly. "Indeed, I'll never forget her arrival and the shock her news caused us."

"She was Muto Kenji's daughter," I said, with renewed sorrow for Kenji's loss. "I cannot believe the Tribe used her so. They wanted to get a child, and once it was born they killed her. I regret it bitterly and I should not have done it, not only because of my son but because it was the cause of her death too. If it is to be my son who kills me, it will only be what I deserve."

"All young people make mistakes," Makoto said. "It is our fate to have to live with their consequences." He reached out and clasped my hand. "I am glad you told me all this. It confirms many things I feel about you, that you have been chosen by heaven and are protected to a certain extent until your goals are achieved."

"I wish I were protected from sorrow," I said.

"Then you would indeed reach enlightenment," he replied dryly.

The full moon brought a change in the weather. The heat lessened and the air cleared. There was even a hint of autumn in the coolness of the mornings. Once the festival was over, my spirits lifted a little. Other words of the abbot came to me, reminding me that my followers, all those who supported me, did so of their own free will. I had to set my grief aside and take up my cause again so that their deaths would not be in vain. And the words Shigeru had spoken to me in a small village called Hinode, on the far side of the Three Countries, also returned to me.

Only children weep. Men and women endure.

We made plans to move on the following day, but that afternoon there was a slight earth tremor, just enough to set the wind chimes ringing and make the dogs howl. In the evening there was another, stronger one. A lamp was knocked over in a house up the street from where we were lodging, and we spent most of the night helping the townspeople contain the ensuing fire. As a result, we were delayed another few days.

By the time we left I was mad with impatience to be with Kaede again. It made me hurry toward Maruyama, rising early and pushing the horses till late at night under the waning moon. We were silent mostly; Jiro's presence was too sharply missed to allow the lighthearted banter with which we had ridden out, and I had a vague sense of apprehension that I could not rid myself of.

It was well into the Hour of the Dog when we reached the town. Most of the houses were already darkened and the castle gates were barred. The guards greeted us warmly, but they could not dispel my unease. I told myself that it was just that I was tired and irritable after the tedious journey. I wanted a hot bath, something decent to eat, and to sleep with my wife. However, her woman, Manami, met me at the entrance to the residence, and as soon as I saw her face I knew something was wrong.

I asked her to tell Kaede I had returned, and she fell to her knees.

"Sir . . . Lord Otori . . ." she stammered, "she has gone to Shirakawa to bring her sisters here."

"What?" I could not believe what I was hearing. Kaede

had gone off on her own, without telling me or asking me? "How long ago? When is she expected back?"

"She left shortly after the Festival." Manami looked as if she would burst into tears. "I don't want to alarm Your Lordship, but I expected her before now."

"Why did you not go with her?"

"She would not allow it. She wanted to ride, to go quickly so she would be back before your return."

"Light the lamps and send someone to fetch Lord Sugita," I said, but it seemed he had already heard of my return and was on his way.

I walked into the residence. I thought I could still smell Kaede's fragrance on the air. The beautiful rooms with their hangings and painted screens were all as she had designed them; the memory of her presence was everywhere.

Manami had told the maids to bring lamps, and their shadowy forms moved silently through the rooms. One of them approached me and whispered that the bath was ready for me, but I told her I would speak with Sugita first.

I went into Kaede's favorite room and my gaze fell on the writing table where she knelt so often to copy the records of the Tribe. The wooden box that held them always stood alongside the table; it was not there. I was wondering if she had hidden it or taken it with her when the maid announced Sugita's arrival.

"I entrusted my wife to you," I said. I was beyond rage, just cold to the depths of my being. "Why did you allow her to leave?"

He looked surprised at the question. "Forgive me," he said. "Lady Otori insisted on going. She took plenty of men with her, led by Amano Tenzo. My nephew, Hiroshi, went too. It was a pleasure trip, to see her family home and bring her sisters here."

"Then why has she not returned?" It seemed harmless enough; maybe I was overreacting.

"I am sure she will be back tomorrow," Sugita said. "Lady Naomi made many such journeys; the domain is used to their mistress traveling in this fashion."

The maid brought tea and food, and we talked briefly of my journey while I ate. I had not told Sugita exactly what I'd had in mind in case it all came to nothing, and I did not go into details now but merely said that I was working out a long-term strategy.

There was no word from the Miyoshi brothers and no

reports on what either Arai or the Otori were up to. I felt as if I were wandering in half-darkness. I wanted to talk to Kaede and I hated this lack of information. If only I had a network of spies working for me . . . I found myself wondering as I had before if it would be possible to find talented children—Tribe orphans, if such children existed—and bring them up for my own purposes. I thought of my son with a strange longing. Would he have a combination of Yuki's talents and mine?

If he did, they would be used against me.

Sugita said, "I hear young Jiro died."

"Yes, sadly. He was struck by an arrow that was intended for me."

"What a blessing Your Lordship escaped!" he exclaimed. "What happened to the assassin?"

"He died. It will not be the last attempt. It is the work of the Tribe." I wondered how much Sugita knew about my Tribe blood, what rumors had been circulating about me during my absence. "By the way, my wife was copying something for me. What happened to the box and the scrolls?"

"She never let them out of her sight," he replied. "If they are not here, she must have taken them with her."

I did not want to show my concern, so I said no more. Sugita left me and I took a bath, calling to one of the maids to come and scrub my back, wishing Kaede would suddenly appear as she had at Niwa's house, and then remembering, almost unbearably, Yuki.

When the maid had left me, I soaked in the hot water thinking about what I was going to tell Kaede, for I knew I must share the prophecy about my son with her, yet I could not imagine how I would frame the words.

Manami had spread out the beds and was waiting to extinguish the lamps. I asked her about the records box and she gave me the same answer as Sugita.

Sleep was a long time coming. I heard the first roosters crow and then fell into a heavy slumber just as day was breaking. When I woke, the sun was well up and I could hear the sounds of the household all around me.

Manami had just come in with breakfast and was fussing over me and telling me to rest after such a long and tiring journey when I heard Makoto's voice outside. I told Manami to bring him in, but he called to me from the garden, not bothering to undo his sandals.

"Come at once. The boy, Hiroshi, has returned."

I stood so quickly that I knocked the tray and sent it flying. Manami exclaimed in shock and started to pick the things up. Roughly, I told her to leave them and bring my clothes.

When I was dressed I joined Makoto outside.

"Where is he?"

"At his uncle's house. He's not in very good shape." Makoto gripped my shoulder. "I'm sorry: The news he brings is terrible."

My immediate thought was of the earthquake. I saw again the flames that we had fought to extinguish and imagined Kaede caught in them, trapped in her burning house. I stared at Makoto, saw the pain in his eyes, and tried to form the unspeakable words.

"She is not dead," he said quickly. "But Amano and all the men, it seems, were slaughtered. Only Hiroshi escaped."

I could not imagine what had happened. No one would dare harm Kaede in either Maruyama or Shirakawa lands. Had the Tribe kidnapped her to strike at me?

"It was Lord Fujiwara," Makoto said. "She is in his house."

We ran across the main bailey, through the castle gates,

down the slope, and over the bridge into the town. Sugita's house lay immediately opposite. A small crowd had gathered outside, staring silently. We pushed through them and entered the garden. Two grooms were endeavoring to persuade an exhausted horse to get to its feet. It was a pretty roan color, its flanks darkened by sweat. Its eyes rolled in its head and froth came from its mouth. I did not think it would ever get up again.

"The boy rode day and night to get here," Makoto said, but I hardly heard him. Even more than usual I was acutely aware of every detail around me: the shine of the wooden floors from within the house, the fragrance of the flowers placed in alcoves, birdsong in the garden shrubs. Inside my head a dull voice was repeating, *Fujiwara?*

Sugita came out at our approach, his face ashen. There was nothing he could say to me. He looked like a man who had already decided to end his life, a shell of what he'd been the night before.

"Lord Otori . . ." he said, faltering.

"Is the boy hurt? Can he talk?"

"You had better come and speak to him."

Hiroshi lay in a room at the back of the house. It gave

onto a small green garden; I could hear a stream flowing through it. It was cooler here than in the main rooms, and the bright morning glare was tempered by shady trees. Two women knelt beside the boy, one wiping his face and limbs with a damp cloth. The other held a tea bowl from which she was trying to persuade him to drink.

They both stopped what they were doing and bowed to the ground when we came in. Hiroshi turned his head, saw me, and tried to sit.

"Lord Otori," he whispered, and despite himself his eyes filled with tears. Struggling to control them, he said, "I'm sorry. I'm sorry. Forgive me."

I pitied him. He was trying so hard to be a warrior, trying so hard to live by the warrior's strict code. I knelt beside him and gently laid my hand on his hair. He still wore it dressed like a child's; he was years from his coming-of-age day, yet he tried to act like a man.

"Tell me what happened."

His eyes were fixed on my face, but I did not return his gaze. He spoke in a quiet, steady voice, as though he had been rehearsing his account over and over on the long ride home.

"When we came to Lady Otori's house, the retainer, Lord

Shoji—don't trust him, he betrayed us!—told the lady that her sisters were visiting Lord Fujiwara. She sent him to bring them back, but he returned saying they were no longer there but the lord would tell Lady Shirakawa—he would only call her that—where they were if she visited him. We went the next day. A man called Murita came to meet us. As soon as Lady Otori rode through the gate, she was seized. Amano, who was at her side, was killed at once. I didn't see any more . . ."

His voice trailed off and he took a deep breath. "My horse bolted. I could not control him. I should have taken a quieter horse, but I liked this one because he was so beautiful. Amano rebuked me for it; he said he was too strong for me. I wouldn't listen. I couldn't defend her."

Tears began to pour down his cheeks. One of the women leaned over and wiped them away.

Makoto said gently, "We must be grateful to your horse. He certainly saved your life, and if you hadn't escaped we would never have known what had happened."

I tried to think of something to say to comfort Hiroshi, but there was no comfort.

"Lord Otori," he said, trying to get up. "I'll show you the way. We can go and get her back!"

The effort was too much for him. I could see his eyes begin to glaze over. I took him by the shoulders and made him lie down. Sweat was mingling with the tears now, and he was trembling all over.

"He needs to rest, but he becomes agitated and tries to get up," Sugita said.

"Look at me, Hiroshi." I leaned over him and let my eyes meet his. Sleep came to him at once. His body relaxed and his breathing evened.

The women could not help gasping, and I caught the look that flashed between them. They seemed to shrink away from me, averting their heads and taking great care not to brush against my clothes.

"He'll sleep for a long time," I said. "It's what he needs. Tell me when he wakes up."

I got to my feet. Makoto and Sugita also rose, looking at me expectantly. Inwardly, I was reeling with outrage, but the numbing calm of shock had descended on me.

"Come with me," I said to Sugita. I really wanted to speak with Makoto alone, but I did not want to risk leaving Sugita. I was afraid he would slit his own belly, and I could not afford to lose him. The Maruyama clan's first loyalty was to Kaede, not to myself; I did not know how they would react to this news. I trusted Sugita more than the rest of them and felt that if he stayed loyal, so would they.

We walked back across the bridge and up the hill to the castle. The crowd outside had increased, and armed men were appearing in the streets. There was an atmosphere of unrest—not really panic or even alarm, just a host of unruly people milling, exchanging rumors, readying themselves for some unexpected action. I had to make decisions quickly before the situation caught fire and burned out of control.

Once we were inside the gates, I said to Makoto, "Prepare the men. We'll take half our warriors and ride at once against Fujiwara. Sugita, you must stay here and hold the town. We'll leave two thousand men with you. Stock the castle against siege. I will leave tomorrow at first light."

Makoto's face was drawn and his voice anxious. "Don't do anything hasty. We have no idea where Arai is. You could be simply riding into a trap. To attack Lord Fujiwara, a man of his rank and status, will only turn opinion against you. It may be best not to react immedi—"

I cut him off. "It's impossible for me to wait. I will do nothing except bring her back. Start at once."

We spent the day in frantic preparation. I knew I was right to act immediately. The first reaction of the Maruyama people was fury and outrage. I wanted to take advantage of that. If I delayed I would seem halfhearted, seeming to accept others' opinion of my legitimacy. I was all too aware of the risks I was taking, and knew I was following one act of rashness with another, but I could not conceive of any other way of acting.

At the end of the afternoon I told Sugita to summon the elders. Within the hour they were all assembled. I informed them of my intentions, warned them of the consequences, and told them I expected their complete loyalty to myself and my wife. None of them made any objections—I think my anger was too strong for that—but I was uneasy about them. They were of the same generation as Fujiwara and Arai and were formed by the same code. I trusted Sugita, but with Kaede gone, could he keep them loyal while I was absent?

Then I called for Shun and went out for a ride on him to clear my head, stretch his legs before taking him on another hard journey, and look at the state of the land.

About half the rice harvest was in, the farmers working day and night to get the rice cut before the weather changed.

Those I spoke to were anxious, forecasting an imminent typhoon, citing the halo around the last full moon, the migrating geese, their own aching bones. I organized Sugita's warriors to lend a hand in strengthening the dikes and banks against floods; no doubt they would complain, but I hoped the sense of crisis would override their pride.

Finally I found myself, only half-intentionally, on the edge of the hamlet where the outcasts had settled. The usual smell of tanning hides and fresh blood hung over it. Some men, Jo-An among them, were skinning a dead horse. I recognized the bright roan color; it was Hiroshi's, the one I'd seen dying that morning. I called to Jo-An and dismounted, giving the reins to one of the grooms who'd ridden out with me. I went and stood by the riverbank and Jo-An came and crouched by the water, washing the blood from his hands and arms.

"You've heard the news?"

He nodded, glanced at me, and said, "What will you do?"

"What *should* I do?" I wanted some word from some god. I wanted to hear another prophecy, one that included Kaede, that bound our futures together. I would follow it blindly.

"There are three more battles," Jo-An said. "One to lose

and two to win. Then you will rule in peace, from sea to sea."

"With my wife?"

He looked away across the water. Two white egrets were fishing near the weir. There was a flash of orange and blue as a kingfisher swooped from a willow. "If you are to lose one battle, you should lose it now," he said.

"If I lose my wife, none of it matters to me," I said. "I would kill myself."

"That is forbidden to us," he replied quickly. "God has his plan for your life. All you have to do is follow it."

When I did not reply, he went on: "It matters to us who have left everything for you. It matters to those in the Otori lands who suffer now. We can bear war if peace comes from it. Don't abandon us."

Standing by the peaceful river in the evening light, I thought that if I did not get her back, my heart would break utterly. A gray heron came flying slowly over the surface of the water, just above its own reflection. It folded its huge wings and landed with the slightest of splashes. It turned its head toward us, watching us, then, satisfied that we posed no danger to it, began to stalk silently through the shallows.

My real goal was to avenge Shigeru's death completely

and take up my inheritance. Then the prophecy would be fulfilled. But it was impossible for me to let anyone take Kaede from me without resistance. I could do nothing but go after her, even if it meant throwing away everything I had struggled for.

I bade farewell to Jo-An and rode back to the castle. Word had come that Hiroshi was awake and improving in health. I asked for him to be brought to me shortly. While I was waiting I searched the residence for the box of records but found no trace of it. It was yet another source of concern. I feared it might have been stolen, which would mean the Tribe had penetrated the castle once and could do so again.

Hiroshi came to me just before nightfall. He was pale, with dark hollows under his eyes, but otherwise he had made a swift recovery. Physically and mentally he was as tough as a full-grown man. I questioned him about every detail of the journey and made him describe the terrain around Shirakawa and Fujiwara's residence. He told me how Raku had been killed, and the news saddened me deeply. The black-maned gray horse was the first I had mastered, a link with Shigeru and my brief life as his son in Hagi. Raku had been my gift to Kaede when I had nothing else to give her, and he had brought her to Terayama.

I'd sent everyone else away so I could speak in private to Hiroshi, and now I told him to move closer.

"Promise you will tell no one what we speak of next."

"I swear it," he said, adding impulsively, "Lord Otori, I already owe you my life. I'll do anything to help rescue Lady Otori."

"We will rescue her," I said. "I leave tomorrow."

"Take me with you," he begged.

I was tempted to, but I did not think he was well enough. "No, you are to stay here."

He looked as if he would protest, but thought better of it and bit his lip.

"The records my wife was copying—did she take them with her?"

He whispered, "We took both the originals and the copies. We hid them at Shirakawa in the sacred caves."

I blessed Kaede in my heart for her wisdom and foresight. "Does anyone else know this?"

He shook his head.

"And you could find them again?"

"Of course."

"You must never tell anyone where they are. Someday we will make a trip together to retrieve them."

"Then we can punish Shoji," he said gleefully. After a moment he added, "Lord Otori, may I ask you something?"

"Certainly."

"The day my father died, the men who killed the guards made themselves unseen in some way. Can you do that?"

"Why do you ask? Do you think I can?"

"The women in the room today were saying that you were a sorcerer—forgive me. But you can do many strange things, like making me sleep." He looked at me, frowning. "It was no ordinary sleep; I saw vivid dreams and understood things I'd never known before. If you can make yourself invisible, will you teach me how?"

"Some things cannot be taught," I said. "They are talents that are born in you. You already have many skills and you have had the best of upbringings."

Something I said made his eyes suddenly fill with tears. "They told me Jiro was dead."

"Yes, he was killed by an assassin who was aiming at me."

"And you killed the assassin?"

"I had him put to death, but he was already dying. He bit off his own tongue."

Hiroshi's eyes gleamed. I wanted to explain something of my pain at Hajime's death and Jiro's, my revulsion at the endless cycle of bloodshed and revenge, but I did not think this warrior's son would be capable of understanding it, even after the Kikuta sleep, and I wanted to ask something else of him.

"Do many people believe I am a sorcerer?"

"Some whisper about it," he admitted. "Mostly women, and idiots."

"I am afraid of disloyalty in the castle. That's why I want to leave you here. If you think there is any danger that Maruyama will side with Arai when I am gone, send word to me."

Hiroshi stared at me. "No one here would be disloyal to Lord Otori."

"I wish I could be as certain."

"I'll ride and find you myself," he promised.

"Just make sure you take a quiet horse," I told him.

I sent him back to his uncle's house and ordered food to be brought. Makoto returned with a report on the preparations; everything was ready for our early departure. However, after the meal he tried again to dissuade me.

"It's utter madness," he said. "I won't say another word after tonight, and I'll go with you, but to attack a nobleman whose betrothed you stole . . ."

"We were legally married," I said. "He is the one who has committed an act of madness."

"Didn't I warn you at Terayama how such a marriage would be viewed by the world? It was your own rashness that has led to this, and it will lead to your downfall if you persist in it."

"Can you be sure you weren't motivated by jealousy then as you are now? You've always resented my love for Kaede."

"Only because it will destroy you both," he replied quietly. "Your passion blinds you to everything. You were in the wrong. It would be better to submit to that and try to make your peace with Arai. Don't forget, he is probably holding the Miyoshi brothers as hostages. Attacking Lord Fujiwara will only enrage him further. . . ."

"Don't give me such advice!" I said in fury. "Submit to having my wife taken from me? The whole world would despise me. I would rather die!"

"We probably all will," he replied. "I am sorry I have to say these things to you, Takeo, but it is my duty to. However, I have told you many times that your cause is mine and I will follow you no matter what you choose to do."

I was too angry to continue talking to him. I told him I wanted to be alone and called to Manami. She came in, her eyes red with weeping, and took away the food trays and spread out the bed. I took a bath, thinking it might be the last for some time. I did not want to stop being angry, for when my rage abated, grief and something worse—apprehension—took its place. I wanted to stay in the intense, dark mood of my Kikuta side that made me fearless. One of Matsuda's teachings came into my mind: *If one fights desperately, he will survive. If he tries to survive, he will die.*

The time had come to fight desperately, for if I lost Kaede, I lost everything.

Manami was even more distressed in the morning, sobbing uncontrollably as she said good-bye and setting off the other maids too. But the mood among the men and in the streets was cheerful, with many townspeople flocking out to shout and wave at us as we rode past. I took only warriors, mainly the Otori and the others who had been with me since Terayama, leaving the farmers to finish bringing in the harvest and to protect their own houses and the town. Most of the Maruyama men stayed to defend the castle, but a few came with us to act as guides and scouts.

I had about five hundred warriors on horseback and perhaps another five hundred bowmen, some mounted and some on foot. The rest were foot soldiers armed with poles and spears. There was a train of packhorses, as well as porters, carrying provisions. I was proud of how quickly my army had been mustered and equipped.

We had not gone far and were about to ford the Asagawa, where we had inflicted such a huge defeat on Iida Nariaki, when I became aware that Jo-An and a handful of outcasts were following us. After the river we took the south road toward Shirakawa. I had never traveled on that road before, but I knew it would take us two days at least to reach Kaede's home, and Makoto had told me Fujiwara's residence lay a short distance farther to the south.

When we stopped for the midday meal, I went to speak to Jo-An, aware as I did so of the glances the men sent in my direction. I set my ears to catch any comments, determined I would punish anyone who muttered anything, but no one dared.

Jo-An prostrated himself at my feet and I told him to sit up. "Why have you come?"

He gave a smile that was more like a grimace, showing his broken teeth. "To bury the dead."

It was a chilling reply, and one I did not want to hear.

"The weather is changing," Jo-An went on, gazing at a mass of high cloud spreading like horses' tails across the sky from the west. "A typhoon is coming."

"Don't you have any good news for me?"

"God always has good news for you," he replied. "I am to remind you of that afterward."

"Afterward?"

"After the battle you lose."

"Maybe I won't lose it!" Indeed I could not imagine it, with my men so fresh and eager and my own rage burning so powerfully within me.

Jo-An said no more but his lips moved silently, and I knew he was praying.

Makoto also seemed to be praying as we rode on, or was

in that state of meditation that monks achieve. He looked serene and withdrawn, as if he had already cut his ties with this world. I hardly spoke to him, as I was still angry with him, but we rode side by side as we had so often done before. Whatever his doubts about this campaign, I knew he would not leave me, and little by little, soothed by the rhythm of the horses' feet, my rage against him abated.

The sky gradually clouded over with a darker tinge on the horizon. It was unnaturally still. We made camp that night outside a small town; in the early hours of the morning it began to rain. By midday it was a downpour, slowing our progress and dampening our spirits. Still, I kept telling myself, there was no wind. We could cope with a little rain. Makoto was less optimistic, fearing we would be held up at the Shirakawa, which was prone to sudden flooding in this weather.

But we never got to the Shirakawa. As we neared the limits of the Maruyama domain I sent scouts ahead. They returned in the late afternoon to say they had spotted a medium-size force, perhaps twelve or fifteen hundred strong, setting up camp on the plain ahead. The banners were Seishuu, but they had also seen Lord Fujiwara's crest.

"He has come out to meet us," I said to Makoto. "He knew what my reaction would be."

"He almost certainly is not here in person," Makoto replied. "But he would be able to command any number of allies. As I feared, they have set a trap for you. Your reaction would not be hard to guess."

"We will attack them at dawn." I was relieved the army was so small. I was not at all intimidated by Fujiwara; what I feared was a confrontation with Arai and some of the thirty thousand men he had under arms. The last I'd heard of Arai was that he was at Inuyama, far away in the east of the Three Countries. But I'd had no news of his activities all summer; he could be back in Kumamoto for all I knew, less than a day's journey from Shirakawa.

I questioned the scouts closely about the terrain. One of them, Sakai, knew the area well, having grown up there. He considered it to be a fair battleground, or would be in better weather. It was a small plain, flanked to the South and East by mountain ranges but open on the other sides. There was a pass to the South, through which our enemies had presumably come, and a broad valley led away to the North, eventually to the coast road. The road we had traveled on from Maruyama joined this valley a couple of miles before the first rocky outcrops of the plain.

There was little water in these uplands, which was why they were uncultivated. Horses grazed on their wild grasses and were gathered together once a year in the autumn. In early spring the grass was burned off. Sakai told me that Lady Maruyama used to come hawking here when she was younger, and we saw several eagles hunting for food before the sun set.

The valley to our rear reassured me. If we should need it, it was a way of retreat. I did not plan to retreat and I did not want to have to fall back to the castle town. My aim was only to go forward, to crush whoever stood in my way, regain my wife, and wipe out the terrible insult of her abduction. However, I had been taught by Matsuda never to advance without knowing how I would retreat, and for all my rage I was not going to sacrifice my men unnecessarily.

No night ever seemed so long. The rain lessened a little, and by dawn it was no more than a drizzle, raising my spirits. We rose in the dark and began to march as soon as it was light, unfurling the Otori banners but not yet sounding the conches.

Just before the end of the valley I ordered a halt. Taking Sakai with me, I went on foot, under cover of the trees, to the edge of the plain. It stretched away to the Southeast in a series of small rounded hillocks covered in long grass and wildflowers, broken by outcrops of strangely shaped gray-white rocks, many of them splashed with yellow and orange lichen.

The rain had made the ground beneath our feet muddy and slippery, and mist hung in swaths above the plain. It was hard to see more than a couple of hundred paces; yet I could hear our enemy clearly: the neighing of horses, the shouts of men, the creaking and jingling of harnesses.

"How far did you go last night?" I whispered to Sakai.

"Just over the first ridge; not much farther than this. Their scouts were also about."

"They must know we're here. Why haven't they attacked already?" I would have expected them to ambush us at the head of the valley; the sounds I heard were those of an army in readiness but not on the move.

"Perhaps they don't want to give up the advantage of the slope," he suggested.

It was true that the slope was in their favor, but it was not particularly steep and gave no huge advantage. The mist bothered me more, as it was impossible to see exactly how many men we faced. I crouched in silence for a few moments, listening. Beyond the drip of the rain and the sighing of the trees I could hear both armies equally . . . or could I? From the enemy the noise seemed to grow in volume like the surge of the sea.

"You saw fifteen hundred at the most?"

"Closer to twelve hundred," Sakai replied. "I'd bet on it."

I shook my head. Maybe the weather, sleeplessness, apprehension, were causing me unnecessary alarm. Maybe my hearing was playing tricks on me. However, when we returned to the main force, I called Makoto and the captains and told them I feared we might be hopelessly outnumbered, in which case we would immediately retreat on the signal from the conch shell.

"Do we pull back to Maruyama?" Makoto asked.

This had been one of my plans, but I needed an alternative. It was what my enemies would expect me to do, and for all I knew they might have already attacked the castle town, in which case I would find myself truly trapped. I took Makoto aside and said, "If Arai has come out against us, too, we cannot stand and fight. Our only hope is to retreat to the coast and get the Terada to transport us to Oshima. If we start to retreat, I want you to ride ahead and find Ryoma. He must arrange it with Terada Fumio."

"They'll say I was the first to flee," he protested. "I would prefer to stay by your side."

"There is no one else I can send. You know Ryoma and you know the way. Anyway, we will probably all be in flight."

He looked at me curiously then. "Do you have a premonition about this encounter? Is this the battle we lose?"

"Just in case it is, I want to preserve my men," I replied. "I've lost so much, I can't afford to lose them too. After all, there are still two to win!"

He smiled; we clasped hands briefly. I rode back to the head of the troops and gave the signal to advance.

The mounted bowmen rode forward, followed by the foot soldiers, with warriors on horseback on either flank. As we came out from the valley, at my signal, the bowmen split into two groups and moved to either side. I ordered the foot soldiers to halt before they came into range of the opposing archers.

Their forces loomed out of the mist. I sent one of the

Otori warriors forward. He bellowed in a huge voice, "Lord Otori Takeo is moving through this country! Allow him to pass or be prepared to die!"

One of their men shouted back, "We are commanded by Lord Fujiwara to punish the so-called Otori! We'll have his head and yours before noon!"

We must have seemed a pitiful force to them. Their foot soldiers, overconfident, began to stream down the slope with their spears held ready. At once our bowmen let fly and the enemy ran into a hail of arrows. Their bowmen retaliated but we were still beyond their range, and our horsemen swept up through the foot soldiers and against the archers before they could set arrow to cord again.

Then our foot soldiers surged forward and drove them back up the slope. I knew my men were well trained, but their ferocity surprised even me. They seemed unstoppable as they rushed forward. The enemy began to pull back, faster than I'd expected, and we raced after them, swords drawn, slashing and cutting at the retreating men.

Makoto was on my right side, the conch shell blower on my left as we crested the hill. The plain continued its undulating roll toward the distant range in the East. But instead of a small army in retreat, we were faced with a far more daunting sight. In the dip between the small hills was another army, a huge one, Arai's western army, its banners flying, its men prepared.

"Blow the conch!" I shouted to the man alongside me. I should have believed my own ears all along. He placed the shell to his lips and the mournful sound rang across the plain, echoing back from the hills.

"Go!" I yelled to Makoto, and he turned his horse with difficulty and urged it into a gallop. It fought the bit, not wanting to leave its fellows, and Shun whinnied to it. But in a few moments we had all turned and were racing after Makoto back to the valley.

I'd been proud of my men's attack, but I was even prouder of them at that moment in the misty autumn dawn when they obeyed the orders instantly and began to retreat.

The swiftness of our turnaround took our enemy by surprise. They had counted on us tearing down the slope after them, where they and Arai's men would cut us to pieces. In the first encounter we had inflicted greater casualties, and for a while their advance was hampered by the fallen dead and by the confusion surrounding both armies. About this time the rain began to fall more heavily again, turning the ground underfoot to slippery mud, which favored us, as we were nearly into the valley with its rockier floor.

I was in the rear, urging the men forward and from time to time turning to fight off our closest pursuers. Where the valley narrowed I left two hundred of my best warriors with orders to hold out as long as they could, buying time for the main force to get away.

We rode all that day, and by the time night fell we had outstripped our pursuers, but with casualties and the rear guard we had left behind, we were barely half the number we had been. I let the men rest for a couple of hours, but the weather was worsening, and as I'd feared, the wind was picking up. So we continued through the night and the next day, hardly eating, hardly resting, occasionally fighting off small bands of horsemen who caught up with us, pushing desperately on toward the coast.

That night we were in striking distance of Maruyama, and I sent Sakai on ahead to see what the situation was in the town. Because of the worsening weather he was of the opinion that we should retreat there, but I was still reluctant to commit myself to a long siege, and still uncertain as to whom the town would side with. We halted for a while, ate a little, and rested the horses. I was beyond exhaustion, and my memories of that time are cloudy. I knew I was facing total defeat—had already been defeated. Part of me regretted not dying in battle in my desperate attempt to rescue Kaede; part of me clung to the prophecy, believing it would still be fulfilled; and part of me simply wondered what I was doing, sitting like a ghost in the temple where we had taken shelter, my eyelids aching and my whole body craving sleep.

Gusts of wind howled round the pillars, and every now and then the roof shook and lifted as if about to fly away. No one spoke much; an air of resigned defiance hung over everyone: We had not quite crossed over to the land of the dead, but we were on our way there. The men slept, apart from the guards, but I did not. I would not sleep until I had brought them to safety. I knew we should be moving on soon—should march again most of the night—but I was reluctant to rouse them before they were rested.

I kept saying to myself, "Just a few more minutes, just until Sakai returns," and then finally I heard the sound of hooves through the wind and the downpour: not one horse, I thought, but two.

I went to the veranda to peer out into the dark and the rain and saw Sakai, and behind him Hiroshi sliding from the back of an old, bony horse.

Sakai called, "I met him on the road just outside the town. He was riding out to find you! In this weather!" They were cousins of some sort, and I could hear the note of pride in his voice.

"Hiroshi!" I said, and he ran to the veranda, undoing his sopping sandals and dropping to his knees.

"Lord Otori."

I pulled him inside out of the rain, gazing at him in astonishment.

"My uncle is dead, and the town has surrendered to Arai's men," he said in fury. "I can't believe it! Almost as soon as you'd left, the elders decided. My uncle took his own life rather than agree. Arai's men arrived early this morning, and the elders caved in at once."

Even though I'd half expected this news, the blow was still bitter, and made worse by the death of Sugita, who had supported Kaede so loyally. Yet I was relieved I had followed my instincts and still had my retreat route to the coast. But now we had to move at once. I called to the guards to rouse the men.

"Did you ride all this way to tell me?" I said to Hiroshi.

"Even if all Maruyama desert you, I will not," he said. "I promised you I'd come; I even chose the oldest horse in the stable!"

"You would have done better to stay at home. My future is looking dark now."

Sakai said in a low voice, "I am ashamed too. I thought they would stand by you."

"I can't blame them," I said. "Arai is vastly more powerful, and we have always known Maruyama cannot sustain a long siege. Better to surrender right away, spare the people, and save the harvest."

"They expect you to retreat to the town," Hiroshi said. "Most of Arai's men are waiting for you at the Asagawa."

"Then maybe there will be fewer in pursuit of us," I said. "They won't expect me to move toward the coast. If we ride day and night, we can get there in a couple of days." I turned to Sakai. "There's no point in a child like Hiroshi disobeying his own clan and throwing his life away on a lost cause. Take him back to Maruyama. I release him and you from any obligation to me."

They both refused adamantly to leave me, and there was

no time to argue. The men were awake and ready. It was still raining heavily, but the wind had dropped a little, renewing my hope that the worst of the storm was over. It was too dark to go at more than an ox's pace. The men in front carried torches that showed the road, but often the rain dimmed them to smoke. We followed blindly.

There are many tales of the Otori, many ballads and chronicles about their exploits, but none has captured the imagination more than this desperate and doomed flight across the country. We were all young, with the energy and madness of young men. We moved faster than anybody could have believed, but it was not fast enough. I rode always at the rear, urging my men forward, not letting anyone fall behind. The first day we fought off two attacks from our rear, gaining precious time for our main force to go forward. Then the pursuit seemed to die away. I imagine no one thought we would keep going, for it was clear by now that we were riding into the whirling heart of the storm.

The storm was covering our flight, but I knew that if it grew any worse, all hope of escaping by boat was gone. On the second night Shun was so tired he could hardly lift one foot after the other. As he plodded along I dozed on his back, sometimes dreaming that the dead rode alongside me. I heard Amano call to Jiro and heard the boy reply, laughing cheerfully. Then it seemed to me that Shigeru rode next to me and I was on Raku. We were going to the castle in Hagi, as we had on the day of my adoption. I saw Shigeru's enemy, the one-armed man, Ando, in the crowd and heard the treacherous voices of the Otori lords. I turned my head to cry out to Shigeru to warn him and saw him as I had last seen him alive on the riverbank at Inuyama. His eyes were dark with pain, and blood ran from his mouth.

"Do you have Jato?" he said, as he had said then.

I snapped awake. I was so wet, I felt I had become a river spirit that breathed water instead of air. In front of me my army moved like ghosts. But I could hear the crash of the surf, and when dawn came it showed us the windswept coast.

All the offshore islands were obliterated by heavy sheets of rain, and with every moment the wind grew stronger. It was howling like a tormented demon when we came to the cliffs where Hajime had lain in wait for me. Two pines had been uprooted and lay across the road. We had to lift them out of the way before we could get the horses through.

I went to the front then and led the way to the shrine of

Katte Jinja. One of the buildings had lost its roof, and thatch was blowing around the garden. But Makoto's horse was tethered in what remained of the building, back turned to the wind, head bowed, alongside another stallion that I did not recognize. Makoto himself was inside the main hall with Ryoma.

I knew it was hopeless before they said anything. In fact, I was amazed that Makoto had made it here at all. That he had found Ryoma seemed like a miracle. I embraced them both, enormously grateful for their loyalty. I discovered later that Ryoma had been told by Fumio to come and wait for me with the message that they would meet me as soon as the weather cleared.

We had not failed through any lack of foresight, courage, or endurance. We had been defeated in the end by the weather, by the great forces of nature, by fate itself.

"Jo-An also is here," Makoto said. "He took one of the loose horses and followed me."

I had hardly thought of Jo-An during our flight to the coast, but I was not surprised to find him here. It was as if I had expected him to appear again in the almost supernatural way he turned up in my life. But at that moment I did not want to talk to him. I was too tired to think of anything beyond gathering the men inside the shrine buildings, protecting the horses as much as possible, and salvaging what remained of our soaked provisions. After that, there was nothing any of us could do but wait for the typhoon to blow itself out.

It took two days. I woke on the night of the second day and realized I'd been dragged out of sleep by silence. The wind had dropped, and though the eaves still dripped, it was no longer raining. All around me men slept like the dead. I got up and went outside. The stars were as bright as lamps and the air clean and cold. I went to look at the horses. The guards greeted me in low voices.

"Weather's cleared up," one said cheerfully, but I knew it was too late for us.

I walked on into the old graveyard. Jo-An appeared like a ghost in the ruined garden. He peered up into my face.

"Are you all right, lord?"

"I have to decide now whether to act like a warrior or not," I said.

"You should be thanking God," he replied. "Now that the lost battle is done with, the rest are for you to win."

I had said the same to Makoto, but that was before the wind and rain had dealt with me. "A true warrior would slit his own belly now," I said, thinking aloud.

"Your life is not your own to take. God still has his plan for you."

"If I don't kill myself, I will have to surrender to Arai. He is on my heels, and there is no way the Terada can reach us before he does."

The night air was beautiful. I heard the muffled whisper of an owl's wings, and a frog croaked from the old pond. The crash of the waves on the shingle was abating.

"What will you do, Jo-An? Will you return to Maruyama?" I hoped uneasily that the outcasts would be well treated when I was no longer there to protect them. With the country in turmoil, they would be more vulnerable than ever, turned on as scapegoats, denounced by villagers, persecuted by warriors.

He said, "I feel very close to God. I think he will call me to him soon."

I did not know how to reply to this.

Jo-An said, "You released my brother from his suffering in Yamagata. If it comes to it, will you do the same for me?"

"Don't say such things," I replied. "You have saved my life; how can you ask me to take yours?"

"Will you? I am not afraid of dying, but I am afraid of the pain."

"Go back to Maruyama," I urged him. "Take the horse you came on. Stay away from the highways. I will send for you if I can. But you know, Arai is likely to take my life. We will probably never meet again."

He gave his characteristic slight smile.

"Thank you for all you have done for me," I said.

"Everything that has happened between us is part of God's plan. You should thank *him*."

I went with him to the horse lines and spoke to the guards. They watched in disbelief as I loosened the stallion's rope and Jo-An leaped onto its back.

After he had trotted off into the darkness, I lay down again but did not sleep. I thought about Kaede and how much I loved her. I thought about my extraordinary life. I was glad I had lived it the way I had, despite all my mistakes. I had no regrets except for those who had died before me. Dawn came as bright and perfect as any I'd ever seen. I washed as best I could and dressed my hair, and when my ragged army awoke, I ordered them to do the same. I called for Ryoma, thanked him for his service, and asked if he would wait at least until he heard of my death and take the news to Fumio at Oshima. Then I gathered the men together and spoke to them.

"I am going to surrender to Lord Arai. In return, I trust he will spare your lives and accept your service. I thank you for your loyalty. No one has been better served than I."

I told them to wait in the shrine under the command of their captains and asked Makoto, Sakai, and Hiroshi to come with me. Makoto carried the Otori banner and Sakai the Maruyama. Both were torn and streaked with mud. The horses were stiff and slow, but as we rode, the sun came up and warmed them a little. A string of wild ducks flew overhead, and a stag barked in the forest. Across the water we could see the clouds above Oshima; apart from them, the sky was a clear, deep blue.

We passed the fallen pines. The storm had gouged out the road around them and undermined the cliff where Hajime had stood. Boulders had tumbled down in a small landslide, and as the horses picked their way around them I thought of the young wrestler. If his arrow had found its mark, Jiro would still be alive—and so would many others. I thought of Hajime's body, lying unburied not far from there: He would soon have his revenge.

We had not gone far when I heard ahead the rapid tramping of horses. I held up my hand and the four of us halted. The horsemen came at a trot, a group of about a hundred, two bannermen carrying Arai's crest at their head. When they saw us in the road they stopped abruptly.

Their leader rode forward. He was wearing full armor and an elaborate helmet, decorated with a crescent moon.

I was thankful for the warmth of the sun, for I was no longer cold and could speak firmly. "I am Otori Takeo. This is Sugita Hiroshi, nephew of Lord Sugita of Maruyama. I ask you to spare his life and return him safely to his clan. Sakai Masaki is his cousin and will accompany him."

Hiroshi said nothing. I was proud of him.

The leader inclined his head slightly, which I took to mean agreement. "I am Akita Tsutomu," he said. "My orders are to bring Lord Otori to Lord Arai. He wishes to speak with you."

"I am prepared to surrender to Lord Arai," I said, "on condition that he spare the lives of my men and take them into his service."

"They may accompany you if they come peacefully."

"Send some of your men with Kubo Makoto," I said. "He will tell them to surrender without a fight. Where is His Lordship?"

"Not far from here. We sat out the typhoon in Shuho."

Makoto left with most of the warriors, and Sakai, Hiroshi, and I rode on in silence with Akita.

· 3 ·

Spring had moved into summer; the planting was finished. The plum rains began; the seedlings grew and turned the fields brilliant green. The rain kept Shizuka inside, where she watched it cascading from the eaves while she helped her grandmother plait sandals and rain capes from rice straw and tend the silkworms in the airy lofts. Sometimes she went to the weaving shed and spent an hour or two at the looms. There was always work to do, sewing, dyeing, preserving, cooking, and she found the routine tasks calming. Though she was relieved to lay aside the roles she had played and glad to be with her family and her sons, often a strange depression took hold of her. She had never been fearful, but now she was troubled by anxiety. She slept badly, woken by the slightest sound; when she slept, she dreamed of the dead.

Kaede's father often came to her, fixing his sightless eyes on her. She went to the shrine to make offerings, hoping to placate his spirit, but nightmares still troubled her. She missed Kaede, missed Ishida, longed for Kondo to come back with news of them, and dreaded his return at the same time.

The rains ended and the hot humid days of high summer followed. Melons and cucumbers ripened and were pickled with salt and herbs. Shizuka often roamed the mountains gathering wild mushrooms, mugwort to make moxa with, bugle and madder for dyes, and the other, deadlier harvest from which Kenji prepared poison.

She watched her sons and the other children at their training, half marveling as the Tribe skills awoke in them. They slipped in and out of sight, and sometimes she saw the trembling, indistinct shape as they learned to use the second self.

Her older son, Zenko, was less skilled than his brother. He was only a year or so away from manhood, and his talents should have been developing rapidly. But Shizuka could see he was more interested in horses and the sword: He took after his father. Would Arai want to own him now? Or would he still seek to protect his legitimate son by removing the illegitimate?

Zenko concerned her more than Taku. It was already obvious that Taku was going to be highly skilled; he would stay with the Tribe and rise high in it. Kenji had no sons, and Taku might even be master of the Muto family one day. His talents were precocious: Invisibility came naturally to him and his hearing was sharp; with the onset of puberty it might even become like Takeo's. He had loose limbs like hers and could fold himself into the smallest of spaces and stay hidden for hours on end. He liked to play tricks on the maids, hiding in an empty pickling barrel or a bamboo basket and jumping out to surprise them like the mischievous tanuki in stories.

She found herself comparing her younger son to Takeo. If her cousin had had the same upbringing, if the Kikuta had known about him from birth, he would have been one of the Tribe, like her children, like herself, ruthless, obedient, unquestioning. . . .

Except, she thought, *I* am *questioning. I don't even think I'm obedient anymore. And what happened to my ruthlessness? I will never kill Takeo or do anything to hurt Kaede. They can't make me. I was sent to serve her and I came to love her. I gave her my complete allegiance and I won't take it back. I told her at Inuyama that even women could act with honor.*

She thought again of Ishida and wondered if gentleness and compassion were contagious and she had caught them from him. And then she thought of the other, deeper secret she held within her. Where had her obedience been then?

The Festival of the Weaver Star fell on a rainy night. The children were dismayed, for the clouded sky meant that the magpies could not build a bridge across heaven for the princess to meet her lover. She would miss their one meeting and be separated from him for another year.

Shizuka took it as a bad omen, and her depression increased.

Occasionally messengers came from Yamagata and beyond. They brought news of Takeo's marriage to Kaede, their flight from Terayama, the outcasts' bridge, and the defeat of Jin-emon. The maids marveled at what seemed to them like something from an ancient legend and made up songs about it. Kenji and Shizuka discussed these events at night, both torn by the same mixture of dismay and unwilling admiration. Then the young couple and their army moved into Maruyama and news of them dwindled, though reports came from time to time of Takeo's campaign against the Tribe.

"It seems he has learned ruthlessness," her uncle said to her, but they did not discuss it further. Kenji had other preoccupations. He did not speak of Yuki again, but when the seventh month passed and no news had come of her, the whole household entered a time of waiting. Everyone was anxious for this Muto child, the master's first grandchild, who had been claimed by the Kikuta and would be brought up by them.

One afternoon just before the Festival of the Dead, Shizuka walked up to the waterfall. It was a day of oppressive heat with no wind, and she sat with her feet in the cool water. The cascade was white against the gray rocks, and the spray caught rainbows. Cicadas droned in the cedars, rasping her nerves. Through their monotonous sound she heard her younger son approaching, though she pretended not to; just at the last moment, when he thought he would surprise her, she reached out and caught him behind the knees. She pulled him into her lap.

"You heard me," he said, disappointed.

"You were making more noise than a wild boar."

"I was not!"

"Maybe I have something of the Kikuta hearing," she teased him.

"I have that."

"I know. And I think it will become even sharper as you grow older." She opened his palm and traced the line that ran straight across it. "You and I have the same hands."

"Like Takeo," he said with pride.

"What do you know about Takeo?" she said, smiling.

"He's Kikuta too. Uncle Kenji told us about him: how he can do things no one else can do, even though he was impossible to teach, Uncle says." He paused for a moment and then said in a small voice, "I wish we didn't have to kill him."

"How do you know that? Did Uncle tell you that too?"

"I heard it. I hear lots of things. People don't know I'm there."

"Were you sent to find me?" she asked, reminding herself to share no secrets in her grandparents' house without checking where her son was first.

"Not exactly. No one told me to come, but I think you should go home."

"What's happened?"

"Aunt Seiko came. She is very unhappy. And Uncle—" He broke off and stared at her. "I have never seen him like that before."

Yuki, she thought at once. She stood quickly and pulled on her sandals. Her heart was pounding, her mouth dry. If her aunt had come, it could only be bad news—the worst.

Her fears were confirmed by the pall of mourning that seemed to have settled over the whole village. The guards' faces were pale, and there were no smiles or banter. She did not stop to question them but hurried to her grandparents' house. The women of the village had already gathered, leaving fires unlit and the evening meal uncooked. She pushed her way through them as they muttered words of sympathy and condolences. Inside, her aunt, Kenji's wife, knelt on the floor next to her grandmother, surrounded by the household women. Her face was drawn, her eyes red, her body shaking with deep sobbing.

"Aunt!" Shizuka knelt before her and bowed deeply. "What happened?"

Seiko took her hand and gripped it hard but could not speak.

"Yuki passed away," her grandmother said quietly.

"And the baby?"

"The baby is well; it's a boy."

"I am so sorry," Shizuka said. "Childbirth . . ."

Her aunt was racked by even fiercer sobs.

"It was not childbirth," the old woman said, putting her arms around Seiko and rocking her like a child.

"Where is my uncle?"

"In the next room, with his father. Go to him. Maybe you can comfort him."

Shizuka rose and went quietly to the next room, feeling her eyes grow hot with unshed tears.

Kenji sat unmoving next to his father in the dim room. All the shutters were closed and it was stifling. The old man had tears trickling down his face; every now and then he raised his sleeve to wipe them away, but her uncle's eyes were dry.

"Uncle," she whispered.

He did not move for a while. She knelt silently. Then he turned his head and looked at her.

"Shizuka," he said. His eyes went bright as tears sprang into them but did not fall. "My wife is here; did you see her?"

She nodded.

"Our daughter is dead."

"It's terrible news," she said. "I am so sorry for your loss." The phrases seemed useless and empty of meaning.

He did not say anything else. Eventually she dared to ask, "How did it happen?"

"The Kikuta killed her. They made her take poison." He spoke as if he did not believe his own words.

Shizuka herself could not believe them. Despite the heat she felt chilled to the bone. "Why? How could they do such a thing?"

"They did not trust her to keep the child from Takeo or to bring him up to hate his father."

She had thought nothing could shock her about the Tribe, but this revelation made her heart nearly stop beating and her voice disappear.

"Who knows, perhaps they also wanted to punish me," he said. "My wife blames me: for not going after Takeo myself, for knowing nothing of Shigeru's records, for spoiling Yuki when she was a child."

"Don't speak of these things now," she said. "You cannot blame yourself."

He was staring into the distance. She wondered what he was seeing.

"They did not have to kill her," he said. "I will never forgive them for that." His voice broke, and though his face was clenched, the tears fell then.

The Festival of the Dead was celebrated with more than usual solemnity and grief. Food was placed at the mountain shrines and bonfires lit on the peaks to light the way back to the world of the dead. Yet the dead seemed reluctant to return. They wanted to stay with the living and remind them over and again of the ways they had died and their need for remorse, for revenge.

Kenji and his wife brought no comfort to each other, unable to draw close in their grief, each blaming the other for Yuki's death. Shizuka spent many hours with each of them, unable to give them any consolation but her presence. Her grandmother brewed calming teas for Seiko, and the woman slept long and often, but Kenji would take nothing to dull his pain, and Shizuka often sat with him until late at night, listening to him talk about his daughter.

"I brought her up like a son," he said one night. "She was so talented. And fearless. My wife thinks I gave her too much freedom. She blames me for treating her like a boy. Yuki became too independent; she thought she could do anything. In the end, Shizuka, she's dead because she was a woman." After a moment he added, "Probably the only woman I've ever really loved." In an unexpected gesture of affection, he reached out and touched her arm. "Forgive me. I am of course very fond of you."

"As I am of you," she replied. "I wish I could ease your grief."

"Well, nothing can ease it," he said. "I will never get over it. I must either follow her into death or live with it as we all must live with grief. In the meantime . . ." He sighed deeply.

The rest of the household had retired. It was a little cooler, and the screens stood open to catch the slight breeze that now and then crept down the mountain. A single lamp burned at Kenji's side. Shizuka moved slightly so she could see something of his face.

"What?" she prompted.

He seemed to change the subject. "I sacrificed Shigeru to

the Kikuta for the sake of unity. Now they have taken my daughter from me too." Again he fell silent.

"What do you plan to do?"

"The boy is my grandchild—the only one I'll ever have. I find it hard to accept that he's lost to the Muto completely. I imagine his father will have a certain interest in him, too, if I know Takeo. I said before that I would not seek Takeo's death; that's partly why I've been hiding out here all summer. Now I will go further: I want the Muto family to come to an agreement with him, to make a truce."

"And go against the Kikuta?"

"I will never do anything in agreement with them again. If Takeo can destroy them, I will do everything in my power to help him."

She saw something in his face and knew he was hoping Takeo would give him the revenge he craved. "You will destroy the Tribe," she whispered.

"We are already destroying ourselves," he said bleakly. "Moreover, everything is changing around us. I believe we are at the end of an era. When this war is over, whoever is the victor will rule over the whole of the Three Countries. Takeo wants to gain his inheritance and punish Shigeru's uncles, but whoever leads the Otori, Arai will have to fight them: Either the Otori clan must conquer or they must be utterly defeated and wiped out, for there will be no peace while they simmer on the border."

"The Kikuta seem to be favoring the Otori lords against Takeo?"

"Yes, I've heard Kotaro himself is in Hagi. I believe in the long run, despite his apparent strength, Arai will not succeed against the Otori. They have a certain legitimacy to claim the Three Countries, you know, because of their ancestral link with the emperor's house. Shigeru's sword, Jato, was forged and given in recognition of that, hundreds of years ago."

He fell silent and a slight smile curved his lips.

"But the sword found Takeo. It did not go to Shoichi or Masahiro." He turned to her and the smile deepened. "I'm going to tell you a story. You may know that I met Shigeru at Yaegahara. I was about twenty-five; he must have been nineteen. I was working as a spy and secret messenger for the Noguchi, who were allies of the Otori then. I already knew that they would change sides during the battle and turn on their former allies, giving the victory to Iida and causing the deaths of thousands of men. I've always been detached from the rights and wrongs of our trade, but the depths of treachery fascinate me. There is something appalling about the realization of betrayal that I like to observe. I wanted to see Otori Shigemori's face when the Noguchi turned on him.

"So, for this rather base motive, I was there in the thick of the battle. Most of the time I was invisible. I have to say, there was something intensely exciting about being in the midst of the fray, unseen. I saw Shigemori; I saw the expression on his face when he realized all was lost. I saw him fall. His sword, which was well known and which many desired, flew from his hands at the moment of death and fell at my feet. I picked it up. It took on my invisibility and seemed to cleave to my hand. It was still warm from its master's grip. It told me that I had to protect it and find its true owner."

"It spoke to you?"

"That's the only way I can describe it. After Shigemori died, the Otori went into a state of mad desperation. The battle raged for another couple of hours, which I spent looking for Shigeru. I knew him: I'd seen him once before, a few years earlier, when he was training in the mountains with Matsuda. It wasn't until the fighting was over that I came upon him. By then Iida's men were searching for him everywhere. If he could be declared dead in battle, it would be convenient for everyone.

"I found him by a small spring. He was quite alone and was preparing to take his own life, washing the blood from his face and hands and scenting his hair and beard with perfume. He had taken off his helmet and loosened his armor. He seemed as calm as if he were about to bathe in the spring.

"The sword said to me, 'This is my master,' so I called to him, 'Lord Otori!' and when he turned I let him see me and held the sword out to him.

"'Jato,' he greeted it, took the sword in both hands, and bowed deeply. Then he looked at the sword and looked at me and seemed to come out of the trance he was in.

"I said something like 'Don't kill yourself,' and then, as if the sword spoke through me, 'Live and get revenge,' and he smiled and leaped to his feet, the sword in his hand. I helped him get away and took him back to his mother's house in Hagi. By the time we got there we had become friends."

"I often wondered how you met," Shizuka said. "So you saved his life."

"Not I but Jato. This is the way it goes from hand to

hand. Takeo has it because Yuki gave it to him in Inuyama. And because of her disobedience then the Kikuta started to distrust her."

"How strange are the ways of fate," Shizuka murmured.

"Yes, there is some bond between us all that I cannot fight. It's mainly because Jato chose Takeo, through my daughter, that I feel we must work with him. Apart from that, I can keep my promise never to harm him and maybe make amends for the role I played in Shigeru's death." He paused and then said in a low voice, "I did not see the look on his face when Takeo and I did not return that night in Inuyama, but it is the expression he wears when he visits me in dreams."

Neither of them said anything for a few moments. A sudden flash of lightning lit the room, and Shizuka could hear thunder rolling in the mountains. Kenji went on: "I hope your Kikuta blood will not take you from us now."

"No, your decision is a relief to me because it means I can keep faith with Kaede. I'm sorry, but I would never have done anything to hurt either of them."

Her admission made him smile again. "So I have always thought. Not only because of your affection for Kaede—I know how strong your feelings were for both Shigeru and Lady Maruyama, and the part you played in the alliance with Arai." Kenji was looking at her closely. "Shizuka, you did not seem completely surprised when I told you about Shigeru's records. I have been trying to deduce who his informant in the Tribe might have been."

She was trembling despite herself. Her disobedience—treachery, to give it its true name—was about to be disclosed. She could not imagine what the Tribe would do to her.

"It was you, wasn't it?" Kenji went on.

"Uncle," she began.

"Don't be alarmed," he said quickly. "I will never speak of it to another soul. But I would like to know why."

"It was after Yaegahara," she said. "I gave the information to Iida that Shigeru was seeking alliances with the Seishuu. Shigeru confided in Arai, and I passed the information on. It was because of me that the Tohan triumphed, because of me that ten thousand died on the battlefield and countless others afterward from torture and starvation. I watched Shigeru in the years following and was filled with admiration for his patience and fortitude. He seemed to me the only good man I had ever met, and I had played a leading part in his downfall. So I resolved to help him, to make amends. He asked me many things about the Tribe, and I told him everything I could. It was not hard to keep it secret—it was what I had been trained to do." She paused and then said, "I am afraid you will be very angry."

He shook his head. "I should be, I suppose. If I had found out anytime before this, I would have had to order your punishment and death." He was gazing at her with admiration. "Truly you have the Kikuta gift of fearlessness. In fact I am glad you did what you did. You helped Shigeru, and now that legacy protects Takeo. It may even make amends for my own betrayal."

"Will you go to Takeo now?"

"I was hoping to have a little more news. Kondo should return soon. Otherwise, yes, I will go to Maruyama."

"Send a messenger—send me. It's too dangerous to go yourself. But will Takeo trust anyone from the Tribe?"

"Maybe we will both go. And we will take your sons."

She gazed steadily at him. A mosquito was whining near her hair, but she did not brush it away.

"They will be our guarantee to him," Kenji said quietly.

Lightning flashed again; the thunder was closer.

Suddenly rain began to fall heavily. It poured from the eaves, and the smell of wet earth sprang from the garden.

The storm lashed the village for three or four days. Before Kondo returned, another message came, from a Muto girl who worked in Lord Fujiwara's residence in the South. It was brief and tantalizing, telling them none of the details they wanted to know, written in haste, and apparently in some danger, saying only that Shirakawa Kaede was in the house and was married to Fujiwara.

"What have they done to her now?" Kenji said, shaken out of his grief by anger.

"We always knew the marriage with Takeo would be opposed," Shizuka said. "I imagine Fujiwara and Arai have arranged this between them. Lord Fujiwara wanted to marry her before she left in the spring. I'm afraid I encouraged her to become close to him."

She pictured Kaede imprisoned within the luxurious residence, remembered the nobleman's cruelty, and wished she had acted differently.

"I don't know what's happened to me," she said to her

uncle. "I used to be indifferent to all these things. Now I find I care deeply; I'm outraged and horrified, and filled with pity for them both."

"Since I first set eyes on her I've been moved by Lady Shirakawa's plight," he replied. "It's hard not to pity her even more now."

"What will Takeo do?" Shizuka wondered aloud.

"He will go to war," Kenji predicted. "And almost certainly be defeated. It may be too late for us to make peace with him."

Shizuka saw her uncle's grief descend on him again. She was afraid he would indeed follow his daughter into death and tried to make sure he was never left alone.

Another week passed before Kondo finally returned. The weather had cleared and Shizuka had walked to the shrine to pray again to the war god to protect Takeo. She bowed to the image and stood, clapped her hands three times, asking also, helplessly, that Kaede might be rescued. As she turned to walk away, Taku came shimmering out of invisibility in front of her.

"Ha!" he said in triumph. "You didn't hear me that time!"

She was astonished, for she had neither heard him nor discerned him. "Well done!"

Taku grinned. "Kondo Kiichi has returned. He's waiting for you. Uncle wanted you to hear his news."

"So make sure you don't hear it too," she teased him.

"I like hearing things," he replied. "I like knowing everyone's secrets."

He ran ahead of her up the dusty street, going invisible every time he passed from sunshine to shadow. *It's all a game to him,* she thought, *as it used to be for me. But at some point in the last year it stopped being a game. Why? What's happened to me? Is it that I learned fear? The fear of losing the people I love?*

Kondo sat with her uncle in the main room of the house. She knelt before them and greeted the man who two months earlier had wanted to marry her. She knew now, seeing him again, that she did not want him. She would make some excuse, plead ill health.

His face was thin and haggard, though his greeting was warm.

"I'm sorry I have been so delayed," he said. "At one point I did not think I would return at all. I was arrested as soon as I got to Inuyama. The failed attack on you had been reported to Arai, and I was recognized by the men who came with us to Shirakawa. I expected to be put to death. But then a tragedy occurred: There was an outbreak of smallpox. Arai's son died. When the mourning period was over, he sent for me and questioned me at length about you."

"Now he is interested in your sons again," Kenji observed.

"He declared he was in my debt, since I'd saved your life. He wished me to return to his service and offered to confirm me in the warrior rank of my mother's family and give me a stipend."

Shizuka glanced at her uncle, but Kenji said nothing.

Kondo went on: "I accepted. I hope that was the right thing to do. Of course, it suits me, being at the moment masterless, but if the Muto family object . . ."

"You may be useful to us there," Kenji said.

"Lord Arai assumed I knew where you were and asked me to give you the message that he wishes to see his sons, and you, to discuss their formal adoption."

"Does he want our relationship to resume?" Shizuka asked.

"He wants you to move to Inuyama, as the boys' mother." He did not actually say *and as his mistress,* but Shizuka caught his meaning. Kondo gave no sign of anger or jealousy as he spoke, but the ironic look flashed across his face. Of course, if he were established in the warrior class, he could make a good marriage within it. It was only when he had been masterless that he'd seen a solution in her.

She did not know if she was more angered or amused by his pragmatism. She had no intention of sending her sons to Arai or of ever sleeping with him again or of marrying Kondo. She hoped fervently that Kenji was not going to order her to do any of them.

"All these things must be considered carefully," her uncle said.

"Yes, of course," Kondo replied. "Anyway, matters have been complicated by the campaign against Otori Takeo."

"We've been hoping for news of him," Kenji murmured.

"Arai was enraged by the marriage. He declared it invalid immediately and sent a large contingent of men to Lord Fujiwara. Later in the summer he himself moved to Kumamoto, close enough to strike at Maruyama. The last I heard was that Lady Shirakawa was living in Lord Fujiwara's house and was married to him. She is in seclusion, virtually imprisoned." He sniffed loudly and threw his head back. "I know Fujiwara considered himself betrothed to her, but he should not have acted in the way he did. He had her seized by force; several of her men were killed—Amano Tenzo among them, which was a great loss. There was no need for that. Ai and Hana are hostages in Inuyama. Matters could have been negotiated without bloodshed."

Shizuka felt a pang of sorrow for the two girls. "Did you see them there?"

"No, it was not allowed."

He seemed genuinely angered on Kaede's behalf, and Shizuka remembered his unlikely devotion to her.

"And Takeo?" she said.

"It seems Takeo set out against Fujiwara and met Arai's army. He was forced to retreat. After that it's all very unclear. There was a huge, early typhoon in the West. Both armies were caught close to the coast. No one really knows yet what the outcome was."

"If Arai defeats Takeo, what will he do with him?" Shizuka asked.

"That's what everyone wonders! Some say he will have him executed; some that he wouldn't dare because of Takeo's reputation; some that he'll make an alliance with him against the Otori in Hagi."

"Close to the coast?" Kenji questioned. "Which part, exactly?"

"Near a town called Shuho, I believe. I don't know the district myself."

"Shuho?" Kenji said. "I've never been there, but they say it has a beautiful natural blue pool, which I've always wanted to visit. It's a long time since I've done any traveling. The weather is perfect for it now. You had both better come with me."

He sounded casual, but Shizuka sensed his urgency. "And the boys?" she asked.

"We'll take them both; it will be a good experience for them, and we may even need Taku's skills." Kenji got to his feet. "We must leave at once. We'll pick up horses in Yamagata."

"What is your plan?" Kondo said. "If I may ask, do you intend to make sure Takeo is eliminated?"

"Not exactly. I'll tell you on the road." As Kondo bowed and left the room, Kenji murmured to Shizuka, "Maybe we will get there in time to save his life."

· 4 ·

No one spoke as we rode, but the attitude of Akita and his warriors seemed courteous and respectful. I hoped I had saved my men and Hiroshi by surrendering, but I did not expect my own life to be spared. I was grateful to Arai for having me treated like an Otori lord, one of his own class, and for not humiliating me, but I imagined he would either have me executed or order me to kill myself. Despite my childhood teaching, Jo-An's words, and my promise to Kaede, I knew I would have no alternative but to obey.

The typhoon had cleared the air of all humidity, and the morning was bright and clear. My thinking had the same clarity: Arai had defeated me; I had surrendered; I would submit to him and obey, doing whatever he told me to do. I began to understand why the warriors had such a high regard for their code. It made life very simple.

The words of the prophecy came into my head, but I put them aside. I did not want anything to distract me from the correct path. I glanced at Hiroshi riding next to me, his shoulders squared, his head high. The old horse plodded calmly along, snorting now and then with pleasure at the warmth of the sun. I thought about the upbringing that had made courage second nature to the boy. He knew instinctively how to act with honor, though I was sorry he had come to experience surrender and defeat so young.

All around us were the signs of the devastation left by the typhoon when it swept along the coast. Roofless houses, huge trees uprooted, flattened rice, and flooded rivers, with drowned oxen, dogs, and other animals stranded among the debris. I felt anxious briefly about my farmers at Maruyama, wondered if the defenses we had built had been strong enough to preserve their fields, and what would happen to them if Kaede and I were not there to protect them. To whom did the domain belong now, and who would look after it? It had been mine for one brief summer, but I grieved over its loss. I had put all my energy into restoring it. No doubt the Tribe would return, too, punish those who had supplanted them, and take up their cruel trade again. And no one but I could put a stop to them.

As we approached the small town of Shuho, Arai's men could be seen foraging for food. I pictured the extra hardship this huge force of men and horses was imposing on the land. Everything that had already been harvested would be taken, and what had not been harvested would have been ruined by the storm. I hoped these villagers had secret fields and hidden stores; if not, they would starve when winter came.

Shuho was famous for its many cold springs, which formed a lake of a brilliant blue color. The water was reputed to have healing qualities and was dedicated to the goddess of good fortune. Perhaps this was what gave the place a cheerful atmosphere, despite the invasion of troops and the destruction of the storm. The brilliant day seemed to promise the return of good fortune. The townspeople were already repairing and rebuilding, calling out jokes to each other, even singing. The blows of hammers, the hiss of saws, set up a lively song against the sound of water as streams ran over-flowing everywhere.

We were in the main street when, to my astonishment, I heard from out of the hubbub someone shout my name.

"Takeo! Lord Otori!"

I recognized the voice, though I could not immediately place it. Then the sweet smell of the fresh-cut wood brought him up to the surface of my mind: Shiro, the master carpenter from Hagi who had built the tea house and the nightingale floor for Shigeru.

I turned my head in the direction of the voice and saw him waving from a rooftop. He called again, "Lord Otori!" and slowly the town's song stilled as one by one the men laid down their tools and turned to stare.

Their silent burning gaze fell on me in the same way that men had stared at Shigeru when he rode back from Terayama to Yamagata, angering and alarming the Tohan who accompanied us, and on me when I had been among the outcasts.

I looked forward, making no response. I did not want to anger Akita. I was, after all, a prisoner. But I heard my name repeated from mouth to mouth, like the buzz of insects around pollen.

Hiroshi whispered, "They all know Lord Otori."

"Say nothing," I replied, hoping they would not be punished for it. I wondered why Shiro was here, if he had been driven from the Middle Country after Shigeru's death, and what news he had from Hagi.

Arai had set up his headquarters in a small temple on the hillside above the town. He was not accompanied by his whole army, of course; I found out later some were still in Inuyama and the rest encamped halfway between Hagi and Kumamoto.

We dismounted and I told Hiroshi to stay with the horses and see that they were fed. He looked as if he were going to protest, then lowered his head, his face suddenly full of sadness.

Sakai put his hand on the boy's shoulder and Hiroshi took Shun's bridle. I felt a pang as I watched the little bay docilely walking beside him, rubbing his head against Hiroshi's arm. He had saved my life many times and I did not want to part with him. For the first time the thought that I might not see him again lunged and hit me and I realized how deeply I did not want to die. I allowed myself to experience this sensation for a moment, then I drew up my Kikuta self like a defense around me, thankful for the dark strength of the Tribe that would sustain me now.

"Come this way," Akita said. "Lord Arai wants to see you immediately."

I could already hear Arai's voice from the interior of the temple, angry and powerful.

At the veranda's edge a servant came with water and I washed my feet. I could do little about the rest of me; my armor and clothes were filthy, coated in mud and blood. I was amazed that Akita could look so spruce after the battle and the pursuit through the rain, but when he led me into the room where Arai and all his senior retainers were gathered, I saw they were all equally well dressed and clean.

Among these large men Arai was the biggest. He seemed to have grown in stature since I had last seen him at Terayama. His victories had given him the weight of power. He had shown his characteristic decisiveness in seizing control after Iida's death, and Shigeru's; he was physically brave, quick-thinking, and ruthless, and he had the ability to bind men to him in loyalty. His faults were rashness and obstinacy; he was neither flexible nor patient, and I felt he was greedy. Whereas Shigeru had sought power because with it he could rule with justice and in harmony with heaven, Arai sought power for its own sake.

All this flashed through my mind as I took one quick look at the man seated on the raised section of the room, flanked by his retainers. He wore elaborate armor, resplendent in red and gold, but his head was bare. He had grown his beard and mustache and I could smell their perfume. Our eyes met for a moment, but I could read nothing in them other than his anger.

The room must have served as an audience room for the temple; beyond the inner doors, which were half-open, I could hear movements and whispers from the monks and priests, and the smell of incense floated in the air.

I dropped to the floor, prostrating myself.

There was a long silence, broken only by the impatient tapping of Arai's fan. I could hear the quickened breathing of the men around me, the beating of their hearts like drums, and in the distance the song of the town rebuilding itself. I thought I heard Shun whicker from the horse lines, the eager sound of a horse seeing food.

"What a fool you are, Otori," Arai shouted into the silence. "I command you to marry and you refuse. You disappear for months, abandoning your inheritance. You reappear and have the audacity to marry a woman under my protection without my permission. You dare to attack a nobleman, Lord Fujiwara. All this could have been avoided. We could have been allies."

He continued in this vein for some time, punctuating each sentence with a thwack of his fan as if he would like to beat me round the head. But his rage did not touch me, partly because I had cloaked myself in darkness, partly because I sensed that it was mostly assumed. I did not resent it; he had every right to be angry with me. I waited, face on the floor, to see what he would do next.

He ran out of rebukes and insults and another long silence ensued. Finally he grunted, "Leave us. I will speak to Otori alone."

Someone to his left whispered, "Is that wise, lord? His reputation . . ."

"I am not afraid of Otori!" Arai shouted, taking rage on again immediately. I heard the men depart one by one and heard Arai stand and step down from the platform. "Sit up," he ordered.

I sat but kept my eyes lowered. He knelt down so we were knee to knee and could speak without being overheard.

"Well, that's out of the way," he said, almost affably. "Now we can talk strategy."

"I am deeply sorry for offending Lord Arai," I said.

"All right, all right, what's past is past. My advisers think you should be ordered to kill yourself for your insolence." To my amazement he began to chuckle. "Lady Shirakawa is a beautiful woman. It must be punishment enough to lose her. I think many are jealous that you went ahead and did what they wished they dared do. And you lived, which many consider a miracle, given her reputation. Women pass, though; what matters is power—power and revenge."

I bowed again, to avoid revealing the fury his shallow words aroused in me.

He went on: "I like boldness, Takeo. I admire what you did for Shigeru. I promised him a long time ago that I would support you in the case of his death; it irks me, as it must you, that his uncles go unpunished. I did speak to the Miyoshi brothers when you sent them. Indeed, Kahei is here with my men; you can see him later. The younger one is still in Inuyama. I learned from them how you outwitted the main Otori army and how many of the clan favor you. The battle at Asagawa was well done. Nariaki had been bothering me and I was pleased to see him removed. We came through Maruyama and saw your work there and Kahei told me how you dealt with the Tribe. You learned Shigeru's lessons well. He would be proud of you."

"I don't deserve your praise," I said. "I will take my own life if you desire it. Or I will retire to a monastery—Terayama, for example."

"Yes, I can see that working," he replied dryly. "I'm aware of your reputation. I'd rather use it myself than have you holed up in some temple, attracting all the malcontents from the Three Countries." He added offhandedly, "You may take your own life if you wish. It's your right as a warrior and I won't prevent you. But I'd infinitely prefer to have you fighting with me."

"Lord Arai."

"The whole of the Three Countries obeys me now, apart from the Otori. I want to deal with them before winter. Their main army is still outside Yamagata. I believe they can be defeated, but they will fall back to Hagi and it is said that the town cannot be taken by siege, especially once the snows begin."

He stared at me, studying my face. I kept my expression impassive, my eyes turned away.

"I have two questions for you, Takeo. How were you able to identify the Tribe in Maruyama? And was your retreat to the coast deliberate? We thought we had you trapped, but you moved too quickly for us, as if it were premeditated."

I raised my head and met his eyes briefly. "I accept your offer of an alliance," I said. "I will serve you loyally. In return I understand that you recognize me as the lawful heir of the Otori clan and will support me in reclaiming my inheritance in Hagi."

He clapped his hands and, when a servant appeared at the door, ordered wine to be brought. I did not tell him that I would never give up Kaede, and he no doubt was less than frank with me, but we drank ceremonially to our alliance. I would have preferred something to eat, even tea. The wine hit my empty stomach like fire.

"Now you may answer my questions," Arai said.

I told him about Shigeru's records of the Tribe and how I had been given them at Terayama.

"Where are they now? At Maruyama?"

"No."

"So where? You won't tell me?"

"They are not in my possession, but I know where they are. And I carry most of the information in my head."

"So that's how you were so successful," he said.

"The Tribe seem eager to assassinate me," I said. "There were not many in Maruyama, but each one represented a threat, so I had to eradicate them. I would have preferred to make use of them; I know what they can do and how useful they can be."

"You will share those records with me?"

"If it helps us both attain our goals."

He sat for a while, brooding on my words. "I was enraged by the part the Tribe played last year," he said. "I did not know they were so powerful. They took you away and managed to keep you hidden while my men scoured Yamagata for you. I suddenly realized they were like damp beneath a house or wood-boring insects that chew away at the foundation of a huge building. I also wanted to wipe them out—but it would make more sense to control them. That brings me to something else I want to talk to you about. You remember Muto Shizuka?"

"Of course."

"You probably know that I had two sons with her."

I nodded. I knew their names, Zenko and Taku, and their ages.

"Do you know where they are?" Arai asked. There was a curious note in his voice: not quite pleading, but close to it.

I did know, but I was not going to tell him. "Not exactly," I said. "I suppose I could guess where to start looking."

"My son from my marriage died recently," he said abruptly.

"I had not heard of it. I am very sorry."

"It was smallpox, poor creature. His mother's health is not good and she took the loss very badly."

"My deepest sympathy."

"I've sent messages to Shizuka to tell her I want my sons with me. I'll recognize them and adopt them legally. But I've heard nothing from her."

"It's your right as their father," I said. "But the Tribe have a way of claiming children of mixed blood who've inherited their talents."

"What are these talents?" he said curiously. "I know Shizuka was an unparalleled spy, and I've heard all sorts of rumors about you."

"Nothing very special," I said. "Everyone exaggerates them. It's mainly a question of training."

"I wonder," he said, staring at me. I resisted the temptation to meet his gaze. I realized suddenly that the wine and my reprieve from death had made me light-headed. I sat still and said nothing, drawing up my self-control again.

"Well, we'll talk about this again. My other question concerns your retreat to the coast. We expected you to fall back to Maruyama."

I told him about my pact with the Terada and my plan to enter Hagi by ship and infiltrate the castle from the sea while sending an army to decoy the Otori forces and tie them up on land. He was immediately taken with the plan, as I knew he would be, and it increased his enthusiasm to tackle the Otori before Hagi was closed by winter.

"Can you bring the Terada into alliance with me?" he demanded, his eyes fiery and impatient.

"I expect they will want something in exchange."

"Find out what it is. How soon can you reach them?"

"If the weather holds, I can get word to them in less than a day."

"I'm trusting you with a lot, Otori. Don't let me down."

He spoke to me with the arrogance of an overlord, but I think we both knew how much power I also held in our transaction.

I bowed again and, as I sat up, said, "May I ask you something?"

"Certainly."

"If I had come to you in the spring and sought your permission to marry Lady Shirakawa, would you have given it?"

He smiled, his teeth white in his beard. "The betrothal had already been arranged with Lord Fujiwara. Despite my affection for Lady Shirakawa and you, your marriage had become impossible. I could not insult a man of Fujiwara's rank and connections. Besides"—he leaned forward and dropped his voice—"Fujiwara told me a secret about Iida's death that very few of us know." He chuckled again. "Lady Shirakawa is far too dangerous a woman to let live freely. I much prefer to have her kept in seclusion by someone like Fujiwara. Many thought she should be put to death; in a way, he has saved her life by his magnanimity."

I did not want to hear any more about Kaede; it made me too angry. I knew my situation was still dangerous and I must not let emotion cloud my judgment. Despite Arai's friendliness and his offer of alliance, I did not completely trust him. I felt he had let me off too lightly and was holding something over me that he had not yet disclosed.

As we stood he said casually, "I see you have Shigeru's sword. May I see it?"

I took the sword from my belt and held it out to him. He received it with reverence and drew it from its scabbard. The light fell on its gleaming blue-gray blade, showing its wave-like patterns.

"The Snake," Arai said. "It has a perfect feel to it."

I could see he coveted it. I wondered if I was supposed to present it to him. I had no intention of doing so.

"I have made a vow that I would keep it till my death and hand it on to my heir," I murmured. "It is an Otori treasure. . . ."

"Of course," Arai replied coolly, not relinquishing the sword. "Speaking of heirs, I will find you a more suitable bride. Lady Shirakawa has two sisters. I'm thinking of marrying the older one to Akita's nephew, but nothing is arranged yet for the younger. She's a beautiful girl, very like her sister."

"Thank you, but I cannot consider marriage until my future is less uncertain."

"Well, there's no hurry. The girl is only ten years old."

He made a couple of moves with the sword, and Jato sang mournfully through the air. I would have liked to have taken it and let it slice through Arai's neck. I did not want Kaede's sister; I wanted Kaede. I knew he was playing with me now, but I did not know where he was leading.

I thought how easy it would be, as he glanced smiling at my face, to fix him with my eyes and, as he lost consciousness, take my sword. . . . I would go invisible, evade the guards, escape into the country.

And then what? I would be a fugitive again and my men, Makoto, the Miyoshi brothers—Hiroshi, probably—would all be slaughtered.

All these thoughts flashed one after the other through my mind as Arai swung Jato over his head. It was beautiful to watch: the heavy man, his face rapt and expressionless, moving so lightly, the sword cutting through the air faster than the eye could see. I was in the presence of a master, no doubt about that, whose skills came from years of practice and discipline. I was moved to admiration and inspired to trust the man in front of me. I would act like a warrior; whatever his commands, I would obey them.

"It's an extraordinary weapon," he said finally, finishing the exercise, but he still did not return it to me. He was breathing slightly more heavily, and tiny beads of sweat had appeared on his brow. "There's one other subject we must discuss, Takeo."

I said nothing.

"There are many rumors about you. The most damaging and one of the most persistent is that you have some connection with the Hidden. The circumstances around Shigeru's death and Lady Maruyama's do nothing to decrease its intensity. The Tohan have always claimed that Shigeru confessed to being a believer, that he would not take the oath against the Hidden or trample on the images when Iida ordered him to. Unfortunately, no reliable witnesses survived the fall of Inuyama, so we will never know for certain."

"He never spoke of it to me," I replied truthfully. My pulse had quickened. I felt I was about to be forced into some public repudiation of my childhood beliefs, and I shrank from it. I could not imagine the choice I was to be faced with.

"Lady Maruyama had a reputation for being sympathetic toward these people. It is said that many of the sect found refuge in her domain. Did you not find evidence of them?"

"I was more concerned with tracking down the Tribe," I replied. "The Hidden have always seemed harmless to me."

"Harmless?" Arai exploded into rage again. "Theirs is the most dangerous and pernicious of beliefs. It insults all the gods; it threatens the fabric of our society. It claims that the lowest of the low—peasants, outcasts—are the equals of nobles and warriors. It dares to say that great lords will be punished after death like commoners and it denies the teachings and existence of the Enlightened One."

He glared at me, his veins blue, his eyes three-cornered.

"I am not a believer," I said. I spoke the truth, but I still felt a pang of regret for the teachings of my childhood and a certain remorse for my faithlessness.

Arai grunted, "Come with me." He swept out of the room onto the veranda. His guards immediately leaped to their feet, one of them bringing his sandals for him to step into. I followed his entourage as he walked swiftly around the side of the blue pool and past the horse lines. Shun caught sight of me and neighed. Hiroshi was standing next to him, holding a bucket. When he saw me, surrounded by guards, his face blanched. Dropping the bucket, he followed us. At that moment I was aware of a movement away to my left. I heard Makoto's voice and, turning my head, saw him ride through the lower gates of the temple area. My men were gathering outside.

A kind of hush fell. I imagine everyone thought I was going to be executed as Arai strode toward the mountain, Jato still in his hand.

Where the rocks rose, a group of prisoners were tied up; they looked like a mixture of bandits, spies, masterless warriors, and the usual unfortunates who were simply in the wrong place at the wrong time. Most of them crouched silently, resigned to their fate; one or two whimpered in terror; one was keening.

Beneath their moans I could clearly hear Jo-An praying under his breath.

Arai called an order and the outcast was pulled forward. I gazed down on him. I had gone cold. I would feel neither pity nor horror. I would simply do what Lord Arai ordered.

Arai said, "I would ask you to trample publicly on the vile images of the Hidden, Otori, but we have none here. This thing, this outcast, was picked up on the road last night, riding a warrior's horse. Some of my men knew him from Yamagata. There was some suspicion then that he was connected with you. He was believed to have died. Now he reappears, having absconded unlawfully from his place of dwelling and, we realize, having accompanied you in many of your battles. He makes no secret of being a believer."

He looked down at Jo-An with an expression of distaste on his face. Then he turned to me and held out the sword. "Let me see how Jato cuts," he said.

I could not see Jo-An's eyes. I wanted to look deep into them, but he was trussed with his head forced down and he could not move it. He continued to whisper prayers that only I could hear, the ones the Hidden use at the moment of death. There was no time to do anything except take the sword and wield it. I knew that if I hesitated for a moment I would never be able to do it and I would throw away everything I'd struggled for.

I felt the familiar, comforting weight of Jato in my hand, prayed that it would not fail me, and fixed my eyes on the exposed bones of Jo-An's neck.

The blade cut as true as ever.

You released my brother from his suffering in Yamagata. If it comes to it, will you do the same for me?

It had come to it, and I was doing what he had requested. I spared him the anguish of torture and gave him the same swift and honorable death as Shigeru. But I still regard his death as one of the worst acts of my life, and the memory of it loosens my teeth and makes me sick to my stomach.

I could show nothing of that then. Any ensuing sign of weakness or regret would have been the end of me. An outcast's death was of less significance than a dog's. I did not look down at the severed head, the gushing blood. I checked the cutting edge of the sword; there was not a trace of blood on it. I looked at Arai.

He met my gaze for a moment before I dropped my eyes.

"There," he said in satisfaction, looking around at his retainers, "I knew we had nothing to worry about with Otori." He clapped me on the shoulder, his good humor completely restored. "We'll eat together and talk about our plans. Your men can rest here; I'll see they're fed."

I had completely lost track of time. It must have been around midday. While we ate, the temperature began to drop and a chill wind sprang up from the northwest. The sudden onset of cold spurred Arai into action. He decided to leave at first light the next day, meet up with the rest of his army, and march at once toward Hagi. I was to take my men back to the coast, contact Terada, and make arrangements for the attack by sea.

We arranged that the battle would take place at the next full moon, that of the tenth month. If I was unable to achieve the sea voyage by then, Arai would abandon the campaign, consolidate the territory he'd taken so far, and retire to Inuyama, where I was to join him. Neither of us put much store by this second plan. We were determined to settle affairs before winter.

Kahei was summoned and we greeted each other with delight, both of us having feared we would never meet again. Since I could not take all my men with me by ship, I would allow them to rest for a day or two before sending them east under Kahei's command. I had not yet spoken to Makoto and was not sure whether to take him with me or send him with Kahei. I remembered he had said he had little experience of ships and the sea.

When I met up with him we were fully occupied with organizing billeting and food in a district already stretched to its limit. I was aware of something in his gaze—sympathy?

compassion?—but I did not want to talk to him or to anyone. By the time everything was settled the best it could be and I returned to the pool, it was early evening. Jo-An's remains were gone. So were all the other prisoners, executed and buried with little ceremony. I wondered who had buried them. Jo-An had come with me to bury the dead, but who would do the same for him?

Since I was passing the lines, I checked on my horses. Sakai and Hiroshi were there, feeding them, glad for their sake as much as their own to have an extra day or so of rest.

"Maybe you should leave with Lord Arai tomorrow," I told Sakai. "We seem to be on the same side as Maruyama again; you can take Hiroshi home."

"Forgive me, Lord Otori," he said, "but we'd prefer to stay with you."

"The horses are used to us now," Hiroshi put in, patting Shun's short, muscular neck as the animal ate greedily. "Don't send me back."

I was too tired to argue about it and, indeed, preferred to keep both my horse and the boy with my own men. I left them and walked toward the shrine, feeling I needed to do something to mark Jo-An's death and the part I had played in it. I rinsed my mouth and hands at the cistern, asked to be cleansed from the pollution of death, and asked for the goddess's blessing, all the while wondering at myself; I seemed to believe in everything or nothing.

I sat for a while as the sun set behind the cedars, staring at the astonishing blue water of the pool. Little silver fish swam in the shallows, and a heron arrived on its great gray wings to fish. It stood in its patient, silent way, its head turned sideways, its black eye unflickering. It struck. The fish struggled briefly and was swallowed.

Smoke from the fires floated upward, mingling with the mist that gathered over the pool. Already the first stars were appearing in a sky like pearl-gray silk. There would be no moon tonight. The wind tasted of winter. The town hummed with an evening song of many men being fed; the smell of cooking drifted toward me.

I was not hungry; in fact, most of the day I'd been battling nausea. I'd forced myself to eat and drink heartily with Arai and his men and knew I should go and join them again soon, to drink more toasts to our joint victory. But I put it off, gazing instead at the pool as the color leached from it and it became as gray as the sky.

The heron, wiser than I was, took off with a clack of wings to go to its roost.

As darkness fell, it seemed I might be able to think of Jo-An without betraying myself. Was his soul now with God, with the Secret One who sees everything and will judge us all? I did not believe such a god existed: If he did, why did he abandon his followers to the suffering the Hidden endured? If he did exist, I was surely damned to hell by now.

Your life has been brought into the open and is no longer your own. Jo-An had believed in this prophecy. *Peace comes at the price of bloodshed.* Despite the teaching of the Hidden not to kill, he had known and accepted that. I was more determined than ever to bring that peace so that his blood, shed by me, would not be wasted.

Telling myself I must not sit there and brood, I was getting to my feet when I heard Makoto's voice in the distance. Someone responded and I realized it was Shiro. In one of those tricks memory plays, I had completely forgotten seeing him earlier. My meeting with Arai and what had happened afterward had laid too thick a layer over it. Now it came back to me, his voice calling my name and the hush that had fallen as I rode through the town.

Makoto called to me. "Takeo! This man was looking for you. He wants you to come to his house."

Shiro grinned. "We've only got half the roof back on. But we've got food to spare and firewood. It'd be an honor."

I was grateful to him, feeling that his earthy practicality was just what I needed.

Makoto said quietly to me, "Are you all right?"

I nodded, suddenly not trusting my voice.

He said, "I am very sorry for Jo-An's death." It was the second time he had used the outcast's name.

"He did not deserve it," I said.

"It many ways it was more than he deserved: a swift death at your hands. It could have been far worse."

"Let's not talk about it; it's done." I turned to Shiro and asked him when he had left Hagi.

"Over a year ago," he said. "Lord Shigeru's death saddened me, and I had no desire to serve the Otori once he—and you—were gone. This is my hometown; I was apprenticed in Hagi as a boy of ten, over thirty years ago now."

"I'm surprised they let you go," I said, for master carpenters of Shiro's skill were usually highly valued and retained jealously by the clans.

"I paid them," he replied, chuckling. "The fief has no money; they'll let anyone go if they give them enough cash in exchange."

"No money?" I exclaimed. "But the Otori are one of the richest clans in the Three Countries. What happened?"

"War, mismanagement, greed. And the pirates haven't helped. Sea trade is at a standstill."

"This is encouraging news," Makoto said. "Can they afford to maintain their army?"

"Barely," Shiro said. "The men are well equipped—most of the fief's income has been spent on armor and weapons— but food is always short and taxes are sky high. There's a lot of discontent. If Lord Takeo returns to Hagi, I reckon half the army will join him."

"Is it common knowledge that I plan to return?" I asked. I wondered what spies the Otori maintained and how soon this news would get back to them. Even if they could no longer afford to pay the Tribe, the Kikuta would no doubt work for them for free.

"It's what everyone hopes," Shiro replied. "And since Lord Arai did not execute you as we all thought he was going to . . ."

"I thought it too!" Makoto declared. "It seemed I arrived to take one last look at you!"

Shiro gazed at the peaceful pool, now dark gray in the fading light. "It would have run red," he said quietly. "There was more than one archer with his bow trained on Lord Arai."

"Don't say such things," I warned him. "We are allies now. I have recognized him as my overlord."

"Maybe," Shiro grunted. "But it was not Arai who climbed into Inuyama to avenge Lord Shigeru."

Shiro and his family—his wife, two daughters, and sons-in-law—made us comfortable in the newly repaired part of the house. We shared the evening meal with them, and then I went with Makoto to drink wine with Arai. The mood was cheerful, even boisterous; Arai was obviously convinced that the last stronghold of opposition was about to fall.

And then what? I did not want to think too much about the future. Arai wanted to see me installed in Hagi, where I would bring the Otori into alliance with him, and I believed he genuinely desired to see Shigeru's uncles pun- ished. But I still hoped to get my wife back, and if I was destined to rule from sea to sea, at some stage I would have to fight Arai. Yet I had now sworn allegiance to him. . . .

I drank savagely, welcoming the sharp comfort of the wine, hoping it would numb my thoughts for a while.

It was a short night. Well before dawn, the first of Arai's troops were stirring, preparing for the long journey. By the Hour of the Dragon they had all departed, leaving the town silent for a while until the sound of repairs took over again. Sakai and Hiroshi had spent the night with the horses— luckily as it turned out, for, to Hiroshi's indignation, two separate warriors had tried to make off with Shun, claiming he was theirs. It seemed his reputation had grown with mine.

I spent the day in planning. I picked all the men who could swim or who knew anything about boats and the sea: all the Otori and some locals who had joined us since we had arrived at the coast. We went through our armor and weapons and equipped the sailors with the best of them. I dispatched spearmen to the forest to cut staves and spears for the men who would march with Kahei. Anyone left over was sent to help rebuild after the storm and salvage as much as possible of the harvest. Makoto set off for the coast to make contact with Ryoma and get details of our plans to the Terada. Arai's land march would take over twice as long as our sea voyage, so we had time in hand to prepare thoroughly.

To my relief the town did have hidden stores that had escaped Arai's hungry men, and they were willing to share these with us. So many sacrifices were being made for me; so much was hanging on this desperate assault. And what about the coming winter? Would these struggles for power simply condemn thousands to starvation?

I could not think about that. I had made my decision. I had to go forward with it.

That night I sat with Shiro and his sons-in-law and talked about building. They had not only worked on Lord Shigeru's house, they had built most of the houses in Hagi and had done all the carpentry for Hagi Castle. They drew plans of the interior for me, filling out what I remembered from the day of my adoption into the Otori clan. Even better, they revealed to me the secret floors, the trapdoors, and the hidden compartments they had installed on Masahiro's orders.

"It looks like a Tribe house," I said.

The carpenters looked slyly at each other. "Well, maybe certain people had a hand in its design," Shiro said, pouring more wine.

I lay down to sleep, thinking about the Kikuta and the Tribe's relationship with the Otori lords. Were they even now lying in wait for me in Hagi, knowing that they did not have to pursue me anymore, for I would come to them? It was not so many weeks since their last attempt on my life, in this area, and I slept lightly, surfacing often to hear the sounds of the autumn night and the sleeping town. I was alone in a small room at the back of the house; Shiro and his family were in the adjoining room. My own guards were outside on the veranda, and there were dogs at every house in the street. It should have been impossible for anyone to approach me. Yet around the darkest time of night I came out of a restless doze to hear breathing in the room.

I had no doubt it was an intruder, for whoever it was breathed in the slow, almost imperceptible way I had been trained in. But there was something different about the breathing: It was light and it did not come from where I would have expected a man's. I could see nothing in the darkness, but I went invisible at once, as the intruder might have better night vision than me. I slipped silently away from the mattress and crouched in the corner of the room.

I could tell from the minute sounds and a change in the feeling of the air that he had approached the mattress. I thought I could smell him now, but it was not the full scent of a man. Had the Kikuta sent a woman or a child against me? I felt a moment of revulsion at having to kill a child, pinpointed where the nose would be, and stepped toward it.

My hands went around his throat, finding the pulse. I could have tightened them then and killed him at once, but as soon as I held the neck I realized it was indeed a child's. I loosened my grip slightly; he had tensed all his muscles to give me the illusion he was thicker built than he really was. Feeling my grip relax, he swallowed and said quickly, "Lord Takeo. The Muto want a truce."

I held him by the arms, made him open his hands, took a knife and a garrote from his clothes, held his nose so he had to open his mouth, and felt inside for needles or poison. I did all this in the dark and he submitted without struggling. Then I called to Shiro to bring a lamp from the kitchen.

When he saw the intruder he nearly dropped the lamp. "How did he get in? It's impossible!" He wanted to give the boy a thrashing, but I restrained him.

I turned the boy's palms over and saw the distinctive line

across them. I struck him in the face. "What are these lies about the Muto when you are marked as Kikuta?"

"I am Muto Shizuka's son," he said quietly. "My mother and the Muto master have come to offer you a truce."

"So why are you here? I'm not accustomed to negotiating with brats!"

"I wanted to see if I could," he replied, faltering a little for the first time.

"Your mother doesn't know you're here? I nearly killed you! What would have happened to the truce then?" I hit him again, but not so hard. "You little idiot!" I realized I sounded just like Kenji. "Are you Zenko or Taku?"

"Taku," he whispered.

The younger one, I realized. "Where's Shizuka now?"

"Not far away. Shall I take you there?"

"At a decent hour of day, perhaps."

"I should go back," he said nervously. "She'll be really angry when she finds I'm gone."

"Serves you right. Didn't you think about that before you took off?"

"Sometimes I forget to think," he said ruefully. "I want to try something and I just do it."

I repressed the urge to laugh. "I'm going to tie you up till morning. Then we'll go and see your mother."

I told Shiro to bring some rope and tied the boy up, instructing one of the shamefaced guards not to take his eyes off him. Taku seemed quite resigned to being a prisoner—too resigned, in fact. I thought he was sure he'd be able to escape, and I wanted to get some sleep. I told him to look at me. Somewhat reluctantly he obeyed, and almost immediately his eyes rolled back and his eyelids closed. Whatever his talents—and I had no doubt they were considerable—he had no resistance against the Kikuta sleep.

That's something I can teach him, I caught myself thinking, just before I, too, fell asleep.

He was still sleeping when I woke. I studied his face for a while. I could see no similarity to me or to the Kikuta; he resembled his mother mostly, but there was a fleeting likeness to his father. If Arai's son had fallen into my hands . . . if the Muto really wanted to make peace with me . . . It wasn't until the relief started to wash over me that I realized how deep had been my dread of a meeting with my old teacher, Kenji, and its outcome.

Taku slept on and on. It did not worry me. I knew

Shizuka would come looking for him sooner or later. I ate a little breakfast with Shiro and sat on the veranda with the plans of Hagi Castle, memorizing them while I waited for her.

Even though I was looking out for her, she was almost at the house before I recognized her. She'd seen me, but she would have gone straight past if I had not called to her.

"Hey, you!" I did not want to name her.

She stopped and spoke without turning. "Me, lord?"

"Come inside if you want what you're looking for."

She approached the house, stepped out of her sandals onto the veranda, and bowed deeply to me. Saying nothing, I went inside. She followed me.

"It's been a long time, Shizuka!"

"Cousin. You'd better not have harmed him."

"I nearly killed him, the little fool. You should look after him better."

We glared at each other.

"I suppose I should check you for weapons," I said. I was extraordinarily pleased to see her and tempted to embrace her, but I didn't want a knife between my ribs.

"I haven't come to harm you, Takeo. I'm here with Kenji. He wants to make peace with you. He's called off the Muto family. The Kuroda will follow, and the others, too, probably. I was to bring Taku to you to prove our good faith. I didn't know he was going to take off on his own."

"The Tribe's record of trust with me is not high," I said. "'Why should I believe you?"

"If my uncle comes, will you talk to him?"

"Certainly. Bring the older boy too. I'll give your sons to my men to look after while we speak together."

"I heard you had become ruthless, Takeo," she said.

"I was taught it by our relatives in Yamagata and Matsue. Kenji always said it was the only thing I lacked." I called to Shiro's daughter and asked her to bring tea. "Sit down," I said to Shizuka. "Your son's asleep. Have some tea and then bring Kenji and Zenko to me here."

The tea came and she sipped at it slowly. "I suppose you have heard of Yuki's death?" she said.

"Yes, I was deeply grieved by the news. And outraged that she should have been used like that. You know about the child?"

Shizuka nodded. "My uncle cannot forgive the Kikuta. That's why he's prepared to defy Kotaro's edict and support you."

"He doesn't blame me?"

"No, he blames them for their harshness and inflexibility. And himself, for many things: Shigeru's death, encouraging you and Kaede to fall in love—maybe for his daughter's death too."

"We all blame ourselves, but fate uses us," I said in a low voice.

"It's true," Shizuka said. "We live in the midst of the world; we can live no other way."

"Do you have any news of her?" I did not want to ask about Kaede. I did not want to reveal my weakness and my humiliation, but I could not help it.

"She is married. She lives in total seclusion. She is alive."

"Is there any way you can contact her?"

Shizuka's face softened slightly. "I am on friendly terms with Fujiwara's physician, and a Muto girl is a maid in the household. So from time to time we hear about her. But there is very little we can do. I dare not make any direct contact. I don't suppose even Kaede fully realizes the danger she is in. Fujiwara has had servants, sometimes even his companions, put to death for no other reason than a dropped tray, a broken plant, or some other misdemeanor."

"Makoto says he does not sleep with her. . . ."

"I believe not," Shizuka replied. "Generally he dislikes women, but Kaede appeals to some part of him. She is one of his treasures."

My teeth ground in rage. I imagined penetrating his mansion at night and seeking him out. I would cut him to pieces, slowly.

"He is protected by his relationship to the emperor," Shizuka remarked, as though she could read my mind.

"The emperor! What does the emperor do for us, miles away from the capital? There might not even be an emperor. It's like a ghost story, made up to frighten children!"

"If we are speaking of guilt," Shizuka said, ignoring my outburst, "I feel I am to blame. I persuaded Kaede to attract Fujiwara. But if it had not been for his support, we would all have starved at Shirakawa last winter."

She finished her tea and bowed formally to me.

"If Lord Otori is willing, I will go and fetch my uncle now."

"I'll meet him here in a couple of hours. I have some arrangements to see to first."

"Lord Otori."

Being addressed thus by Shizuka had a strange effect on me, for I had only heard her use the name before to Shigeru. I realized that during the course of our meeting I had progressed from *Cousin* to *Takeo* to *Lord Otori*. Irrationally it pleased me. I felt that if Shizuka recognized my authority, it must be real.

I told my guards to keep an eye on Taku and went to check out what remained of my army. The two days of rest and decent food had done wonders for both men and horses. I was anxious to move back to the coast, to hear from Fumio as soon as possible, and thought I would ride there with a small group, but I was unsure what to do with the rest of the troops. The problem as always was one of food. The Shuho people had been generous to us, but to expect them to continue to feed us was stretching their goodwill and their resources. Even if I sent the bulk of the army now, under Kahei's command, to follow Arai by the land route, I needed provisions for them.

I was mulling over these problems as I returned to Shiro's house at midday. I recalled the fisherman on the beach and the bandits he had been afraid of. A sortie against bandits might be just the thing to fill in time, keep the men from idleness, restore their fighting spirit after our retreat, please the local people, and possibly obtain more provisions and equipment. The idea appealed to me enormously.

A man was squatting on his heels in the shadow of the tile roof—an unremarkable man, wearing faded blue-gray clothes and carrying no visible weapon. A boy about twelve years old was beside him. They both stood up slowly when they saw me.

I made a movement with my head. "Come up."

Kenji stepped out of his sandals onto the veranda.

"Wait here," I told him. "Let the boy come with me." I went inside with Zenko to where Taku still slept. I took Taku's own garrote and told the guards to strangle the boys with it if any attack was made on me. Zenko said nothing and made no sign of fear. I could see how like Arai he was. Then I went back to my teacher.

Once we were inside the house, we both sat down. We studied each other for a moment, then Kenji bowed and said in his ironic way, "Lord Otori."

"Muto," I replied. "Taku is also in the next room. He and his brother will die immediately if there is any attempt made on my life."

Kenji looked older, and I saw a weariness in his face that had not been there before. His hair was beginning to gray at the temples.

"I have no desire to harm you, Takeo." He saw my frown and amended his words somewhat impatiently: "Lord Otori. You probably won't believe me, but I never did. I meant it that night at Shigeru's when I vowed I would protect you while I lived."

"You have a strange way of keeping your promises," I said.

"I think we all know what it's like to be torn between conflicting obligations," he said. "Can we put that behind us now?"

"I would be glad if we were no longer enemies." I was acting more coldly than I felt, constrained by all that had happened between my old teacher and myself. For a long time I'd held him partly responsible for Shigeru's death; now my resentment was melted by sorrow for Yuki's death, for his grief. But I was not proud of myself in relation to Yuki, and then there was the question of the child, my son, his grandson.

Kenji sighed. "The situation's become intolerable. What's the point of wiping each other out? The reason the Kikuta claimed you in the first place was to try to preserve your talents. If anyone ever spat upward it was them! I know you have the records that Shigeru kept. I don't doubt that you can deal a terrible blow to the Tribe."

"I would rather work with the Tribe than destroy them," I said. "But their loyalty to me must be total. Can you guarantee that?"

"I can for all except the Kikuta. They will never be reconciled to you." He said nothing for a moment, then continued bleakly: "Nor I to them."

I said, "I am very sorry about your daughter. I blame myself terribly for her death. I can make no excuse. I just wish I could say that if I had my life over again, I would act differently."

"I don't blame you," Kenji said. "Yuki chose you. I blame myself because I brought her up to believe she had more freedom than she really did. Ever since she brought Jato to you, the Kikuta doubted her obedience to them. They were afraid she would influence the child. He is to hate you, you understand. The Kikuta are very patient. And Yuki did not hate you and never would. She always took your part." He smiled painfully. "She was very angry when we took you at

Inuyama. She told me it would never work out to keep you against your will."

I felt the corners of my eyes grow hot.

"She loved you," Kenji said. "Perhaps you would have loved her if you had not already met Lady Shirakawa. I blame myself for that too. I actually arranged your meeting. I watched you fall in love with her during the training session. Why, I don't know. Sometimes I think we were all bewitched on that journey."

I thought so, too, remembering the pelting rain, the intensity of my passion for Kaede, the madness of my foray into Yamagata Castle, Shigeru's journey toward death.

"I might wish things had been different, Takeo, but I don't blame you or hold any grudge against you."

I did not pick him up on his familiarity this time. He went on, sounding more like my old teacher: "You often act like an idiot, but fate seems to be using you for some purpose, and our lives are bound together in some way. I'm prepared to entrust Zenko and Taku to you as a sign of my good faith."

"Let's drink to it," I said, and called to Shiro's daughter to bring wine.

When she had poured it and gone back to the kitchen, I said, "Do you know where my son is?" I found it hard to imagine the child, a baby, motherless.

"I've been unable to find out. But I suspect Akio may have taken him north, beyond the Three Countries. I suppose you will try to find him?"

"When all this is over." I was tempted to tell Kenji about the prophecy, that my own son would destroy me, but in the end I kept it to myself.

"It seems that the Kikuta master Kotaro is in Hagi," Kenji told me as we drank.

"Then we will meet there. I hope you will come with me."

He promised he would and we embraced.

"What do you want to do with the boys?" Kenji said. "Will you keep them here with you?"

"Yes. Taku seems to be very talented. Would you send him alone on a spying mission? I might have a job for him."

"Into Hagi? That would be a bit beyond him."

"No, just locally. I want to track down some bandits."

"It's unknown territory to him around here. He'd probably get lost. What do you want to find out?"

"How many they are, what their stronghold's like, that sort of thing. He has invisibility, doesn't he? He wouldn't have got past my guards without it."

Kenji nodded. "Maybe Shizuka can go with him. But is there a local person who can accompany them at least some of the way? It would save a lot of time on the mountain."

We asked Shiro's daughters and the younger one said she would go. She often went out to collect mushrooms and wild plants for food and medicine, and though she avoided the bandits' area, she knew the countryside all the way to the coast.

Taku woke up as we were talking. The guards called to me, and Kenji and I went in to see him. Zenko still sat where I had left him, unmoving.

Taku grinned at us and exclaimed, "I saw Hachiman in a dream!"

"That's good," I told him, "because you are going to war!"

He and Shizuka went out that night and returned with all the information I needed. Makoto came back from the coast just in time to accompany me as we took two hundred men and stormed the rocky hideout, with so few losses I could hardly describe it as a battle. The results were all I'd hoped for: all the bandits dead, save two who were captured alive, and their winter provisions ours. We set free a number of women who had been abducted, among them the mother and sisters of the child I had fed on the beach. Zenko came with us and fought like a man, and Taku proved invaluable: Even his mother gave him a word of praise. Word spread quickly to the fishing villages that I had returned and kept my promise to the fisherman. Everyone came to offer their boats to help transport my men.

I told myself all this activity was to keep my men from idleness, but in fact it was as much for my own sake. Speaking to Shizuka about Kaede and hearing of her intolerable plight intensified my longing for her a thousandfold. I was busy enough in the day to keep my thoughts at bay, but at night they returned to torment me. All week there were small earth tremors. I had the enduring vision of her trapped in a shaking building as it collapsed and burned. I was riven by anxiety: that she should die, that she should think I had abandoned her, that I would die without telling her how much I loved her and would never love anyone but her. The knowledge that Shizuka could possibly get a message to her kept returning to me with needling intensity.

Taku and Hiroshi formed a somewhat stormy relationship, being about the same age but total opposites in upbringing and character. Hiroshi disapproved of Taku and was jealous of him. Taku teased him with Tribe tricks that infuriated him. I was too busy to mediate between them, but they followed me around most of the time, squabbling like dogs. The older boy, Zenko, kept aloof from both of them. I knew his Tribe talents were slight, but he was good with horses and already an expert with the sword. He also seemed to have been trained perfectly in obedience. I was not sure what I would do with him in the future, but he was Arai's heir and I knew I would have to come to a decision about him sooner or later.

We held a great feast to bid farewell to the people of Shuho, and then, with the food supplied by the bandits, Kahei, Makoto, and my main force set out to march to Hagi. I sent Hiroshi with them, silencing his protests by telling him he could ride Shun, and hoping the horse would take as good care of him as he had of me.

It was hard to say good-bye to them all, especially to Makoto. My closest friend and I held each other in a long embrace. I wished we were going into battle together, but he had no knowledge of boats and I needed him to command the land army with Kahei.

"We will meet in Hagi," we promised each other.

Once they were gone, I felt I needed to keep informed about their movements, about Arai's progress, and about the situation in Maruyama and at Lord Fujiwara's residence. I wanted to know the nobleman's reaction to my new alliance with Arai. Now I could start using the Muto Tribe network.

Kondo Kiichi had accompanied Shizuka and Kenji to Shuho, and I realized he could also be useful to me, being now in Arai's service. Arai and Fujiwara were, after all, allies, which gave Kondo an excuse to approach the nobleman directly. Shizuka told me that Kondo was essentially a pragmatic and obedient man who would serve whomever he was told to by Kenji. He seemed to have no problems with swearing allegiance to me. With Kenji's agreement, Kondo and Shizuka set out to make contact with their Muto spies in the Southwest. Before they left, I drew Shizuka aside and gave her a message to pass on to Kaede: that I loved her, that I would come for her soon, that she should be patient, that she must not die before I saw her again.

"It's dangerous, especially to Kaede herself," Shizuka said.

"I'll do what I can, but I can't promise anything. But we will send messages back to you before the full moon."

I returned to the deserted shrine on the coast and set up camp there. A week passed; the moon entered into the first quarter. We had our first message from Kondo: Arai had encountered the Otori army near Yamagata, and it was in retreat toward Hagi. Ryoma returned from Oshima to say the Terada were ready. The weather held fair, the seas calm, apart from the earthquakes, which caused large swells, increasing my sense of urgency.

Two days before the full moon, at midday, we saw dark shapes in the distance coming from Oshima: It was the fleet of pirate ships. There were twelve of them, enough with the fishing boats to take all my remaining men. I lined my warriors up on the shore, ready to embark.

Fumio leaped out of the leading boat and waded through the water toward me. One of his men followed him carrying a long bundle and two smaller baskets. After we embraced he said, "I've brought something to show you. Take me inside; I don't want everyone to see it."

We went inside the shrine while his sailors began directing the embarkation. The man put the bundles down and went to sit on the edge of the veranda. I could already guess from the smell what one of the objects was, and I wondered why Fumio should have gone to the bother of bringing someone's head to me, and whose it was.

He unwrapped it first. "Look at it and then we'll bury it. We took a ship a couple of weeks ago with this man on it— one of several."

I looked at the head with distaste. The skin was white as pearl and the hair yellow like the yolk of a bird's egg. The features were large, the nose hooked.

"Is it a man or a demon?"

"It's one of the barbarians that made the seeing tube."

"Is that what's in there?" I indicated the long bundle.

"No! Something much more interesting!" Fumio unwrapped the object and showed it to me. I took it warily.

"A weapon?" I wasn't sure how you wielded it, but it had the unmistakable look of something designed to kill.

"Yes, and I think we can copy it. I've had another one made already. Not quite right—it killed the man who was testing it—but I think I know where we went wrong." His eyes were gleaming, his face alight.

"What does it do?"

"I'll show you. Do you have someone you can dispense with?"

I thought of the two bandits we had taken. They had been pegged out on the beach, an example to anyone else who might be considering their calling, and given just enough water to keep them alive. I'd heard their groans while we were waiting for Fumio and thought I must do something about them before we left.

Fumio called to his man, who brought a pan of coals. We had the bandits, pleading and cursing, tied upright to trees. Fumio walked about fifty or sixty paces down the beach, signaling to me to go with him. He lit a cord from the coals and applied the smoldering end to one end of the tube. It had a kind of hook, like a spring. He held the tube up, squinting along it toward the prisoners. There was a sudden sharp noise, which made me jump, and a puff of smoke. The bandit gave one fierce cry. Blood was pouring from a wound in his throat. He was dead within seconds.

"Ah," Fumio said with satisfaction, "I'm getting the hang of it."

"How long before you can shoot again?" I asked. The weapon was crude and ugly. It had none of the beauty of the sword, none of the majesty of the bow, but I could see that it would be more effective than either.

He went through the process again and I counted my breaths: over one hundred, a long time in the middle of a battle. The second shot hit the other bandit in the chest, tearing a sizable hole. I guessed the ball would penetrate most armor. The possibilities of the weapon both intrigued and repelled me.

"Warriors will call it a coward's weapon," I said to Fumio.

He laughed. "I don't mind fighting the coward's way if it means I survive!"

"You'll bring it with you?"

"If you promise to destroy it if we lose." He grinned. "No one else must learn how to make them."

"We are not going to lose. What do you call it?"

"A firearm," he replied.

We went back inside and Fumio rewrapped the firearm. The hideous head stared with blind eyes. Flies were beginning to settle on it, and the smell seemed to permeate the whole room, nauseating me.

"Take it away," I ordered the pirate. He looked at his master.

"I'll just show you his other things." Fumio took the third bundle and unwrapped it. "He wore this round his neck."

"Prayer beads?" I said, taking the white string. The beads looked like ivory. The string unraveled and the sign the Hidden use, the cross, fell into the air before my eyes. It shocked me to see so openly displayed something that for me had always been the deepest secret. In our priest's house in Mino the windows were set so that at certain times of day the sun formed a golden cross on the wall, but that fleeting image was the only one I'd seen before.

Keeping my face impassive, I tossed the beads back to Fumio. "Strange. Some barbarian religion?"

"You are an innocent, Takeo. This is the sign the Hidden worship."

"How do you know?"

"I know all sorts of things," he said impatiently. "I'm not afraid of knowledge. I've been to the mainland. I know the world is much larger than our string of islands. The barbarians share the beliefs of the Hidden. I find that fascinating."

"No use in battle, though!" I found it not so much fascinating as alarming, as though it were some sinister message from a god I no longer believed in.

"But what else do they have, the barbarians? Takeo, when you are established in Hagi, send me to them. Let's trade with them. Let's learn from them."

It was hard for me to imagine that future. All I could think about was the coming struggle.

By midafternoon the last of the men were on board. Fumio told me we had to leave to catch the evening tide. I put Taku on my shoulders, and Kenji, Zenko, and I waded out to Fumio's boat and were pulled over the gunwales. The fleet was already under way, the yellow sails catching the breeze. I stared at the land as it became smaller and smaller and then faded into the mist of evening. Shizuka had said she would send messages before we left, but we had heard nothing from her. Her silence added to my anxiety, for her and for Kaede.

Rieko's disposition was nervous, and she was as alarmed by the typhoon as she had been by the earthquake. It threw her into a state of near collapse. Despite the discomfort of the storm, Kaede was grateful to be free of the woman's constant attention. However, after two days the wind dropped, clear autumn weather followed, and Rieko recovered her health and strength along with her aggravating attentiveness.

She seemed to find something to do to Kaede every day, plucking her eyebrows, scrubbing her skin with rice bran, washing and combing her hair, powdering her face to an unnatural whiteness, creaming her hands and feet until they were as smooth and translucent as pearl. She selected Kaede's clothes for her and dressed her with the help of the maids. Occasionally, as a special privilege, she would read a little to her or play the lute—at which, as she let Kaede know, she was considered to be highly skilled.

Fujiwara visited once a day. Kaede was instructed by Rieko in the art of making tea and she prepared it for him, going silently through the ritual while he followed every movement, correcting her from time to time. On fine days the women sat in a room that looked out onto a small enclosed garden. Two twisted pine trees and a plum tree of extreme antiquity grew there along with azaleas and peonies.

"We will enjoy the flowers in the spring," Rieko said, for the shrubs were a dull autumn green, and Kaede thought of the long winter that stretched ahead and after that another and another, reducing her to a lifeless treasure, seen only by Lord Fujiwara.

The garden reminded her of the one at Noguchi Castle where she had sat briefly with her father when he had been informed of the marriage arranged with Lord Otori Shigeru. He had been proud then, relieved that she was to make such a good marriage. Neither of them had known that that marriage, too, would be a sham, a trap for Shigeru. Since she had so little with which to occupy her thoughts, she went over and over the past in her mind while she gazed out on the garden, watching every minute change as the days went slowly by.

The plum tree began to drop its leaves and an old man came into the garden to pick them one by one off the moss. Kaede had to be kept out of his sight, as from all men, but she watched him from behind a screen. With infinite patience he picked up each leaf between finger and thumb so the moss would not be damaged and placed it in a bamboo basket. Then he combed the moss as if it were hair, removing every scrap of twig and grass, worm castings, birds' feathers, pieces of bark. For the rest of the day the moss looked pristine, and then slowly, imperceptibly, the world, life, began to encroach on it, and the next morning the process began again.

Green and white lichen grew on the gnarled trunk and branches of the plum tree, and Kaede found herself watching that too every day. Tiny events had the power to startle her. One morning an ivory-marbled pale pink fungus like a flower carved from flesh had erupted in the moss, and when occasionally a bird alighted on the top of one of the pine trees and let out a trill of song, her pulse stammered in response.

Running a domain had not fully occupied her restless, hungry mind; now she had so little to do, she thought she would die of boredom. She tried to hear the rhythm of the household beyond the walls of her rooms, but few sounds penetrated to the solitary place. Once she heard the cadence of a flute and thought it might be Makoto. She dreaded seeing him, for she was gripped with jealousy at the thought of him free to come and go, free to be with Takeo and fight alongside him; yet she longed to see him, to have some news, any news. But she had no way of knowing if it was the young monk or not.

After the boredom, the worst thing was knowing nothing. Battles might be fought and lost, warlords might rise and fall—all news was kept from her. Her one consolation was that if Takeo were dead, she felt Fujiwara would tell her, taunting her with it, taking pleasure in his death and her suffering.

She knew Fujiwara continued to have his plays performed and wondered sometimes if he had written her own story as he had once suggested. Mamoru frequently accompanied him on his visits and was reminded to study Kaede's expressions and copy them. She was not permitted to watch the dramas, but she could hear snatches of words and chanting, the sounds of the musicians, the beating of a drum. Occasionally she would catch a phrase that she was familiar with and the play it came from would take shape in her head and she would find herself suddenly moved to tears by the beauty of the words and the poignancy of the emotions.

Her own life seemed just as poignant, just as moving. Forced to contemplate the tiny details of her present existence, she began to seek ways to capture her own feelings. Words came to her one by one. Sometimes it took her all day to select them. She knew little of formal poetry, other than that which she had read in her father's books, but she collected words like golden beads and strung them together in ways that pleased her. She kept them secret inside her own heart.

She came to love above everything the silence in which the poems formed themselves, like the pillars in the sacred caves of Shirakawa, drip by drip from the limy water. She resented Rieko's chatter, a mixture of malice and self-importance expressed in commonplaces, and Fujiwara's visits, his contrived artificiality, which seemed the complete opposite of the unadorned truth that she sought. Apart from Fujiwara, the only man she saw was Ishida. The physician came every few days and she enjoyed his visits, though they hardly spoke to each other. When she started looking for words, she stopped taking the calming teas; she wanted to know her feelings, no matter what the anguish.

Next to the room that gave onto the garden was a small household shrine with statues of the Enlightened One and the all-merciful Kannon. Not even Rieko dared to prevent Kaede from praying, and she knelt there for many hours until she entered a state where prayer and poetry became one and the everyday world seemed full of holiness and significance. She meditated often on the thoughts that had disturbed her after the battle of Asagawa and Takeo's persecution of the Tribe, and wondered if this state of holiness that she brushed against might bring an answer on how to rule without resorting to violence. Then she chided herself, for she could not see how she would ever rule again, and she had to admit that if she were to wield power she would seek revenge on all those who had inflicted suffering upon her.

Lamps burned day and night before the shrine, and often Kaede lit incense and let its heavy fragrance fill her nostrils and permeate the air around her. A small bell hung from a frame, and from time to time she would feel the impulse to strike it sharply. The clear note echoed through her rooms, and the maids exchanged glances, careful not to let Rieko see them. They knew something of Kaede's history, pitied her, and increasingly admired her.

One of these girls in particular interested Kaede. She knew from the records that she had copied for Takeo that several Tribe members were employed in Fujiwara's household, almost certainly unknown to him. Two men, one of them the estate steward, were paid from the capital; presumably they were spies placed there to report back to the court on the exiled nobleman's activities. There were two servants in the kitchen who sold snippets of information to whoever would pay them, and another woman, a maid, whom Kaede had tentatively identified as this girl.

She had little to go on beyond the fact that there was something indefinable about her that reminded her of Shizuka and that the girl's hands were similar in shape. Kaede had not missed Shizuka when they had first separated; her life had been completely taken up with Takeo. But now, in the company of women, she missed her acutely. She longed to hear her voice and yearned for her cheerfulness and courage.

Above all, she longed for news. The girl's name was Yumi. If anyone knew what was happening in the outside world, it would be one of the Tribe, but Kaede was never alone with her and was afraid to approach her even indirectly. At first she thought the girl might have been sent to assassinate her, for some motive of revenge or to punish Takeo, and she watched her without seeming to, not out of fear but rather with a sort of curiosity: how it would be done, what it would feel like, and if her first response would be relief or regret.

She knew the sentence of death the Tribe had passed on Takeo, made more stringent by the rigors with which he had pursued them in Maruyama. She did not expect any sympathy or support from them. And yet there was something in the girl's demeanor that suggested she was not hostile to Kaede.

As the days grew shorter and cooler, winter garments were brought out and aired, summer ones washed, folded, and put away. For two weeks Kaede wore the in-between season robes and found herself grateful for their extra warmth. Rieko and the maids sewed and embroidered, but Kaede was not allowed to take part. She did not particularly like sewing—she had had to struggle with her left-handedness to become deft at it—but it would have helped fill the empty days. The colors of the thread appealed to her, and she was enchanted by the way a flower or bird came alive against the heavy silk fabric. She gathered from Rieko that Lord Fujiwara had ordered all needles, scissors, and knives to be kept from her. Even mirrors had to be brought to her only by Rieko. Kaede thought of the tiny needle-size weapon Shizuka had fashioned for her and hidden in her sleeve hem and the use she had put it to at Inuyama. Did Fujiwara really fear that she might do the same to him?

Rieko never let Kaede out of her sight, except when Fujiwara paid his daily visit. She accompanied her to the bathhouse and even to the privy, where she held the heavy robes aside and afterward washed Kaede's hands for her at the cistern. When Kaede's bleeding began, Fujiwara ceased his visits until she had been purified at the end of the week.

Time went past. The plum tree was bare. One morning the moss and the pine needles had a glimmer of frost. The onset of the cold weather brought a wave of sickness. First Kaede caught a cold; her head ached and her throat felt as if she had swallowed needles. The fever brought disturbing dreams, but after a few days she recovered, apart from a cough that troubled her at night. Ishida gave her willow bark and valerian. By that time Rieko had caught the cold; it seemed to have increased in virulence, and the older woman was far more ill than Kaede had been.

On the third evening of Rieko's illness there came a series of small earth tremors. These and the fever sent Rieko into a state of panic. She became almost uncontrollable. Alarmed, Kaede sent Yumi to fetch Ishida.

Night had fallen by the time he arrived; a silver three-quarter moon hung in an intensely black sky, and the stars were icy points of light.

Ishida told Yumi to bring hot water and he brewed a strong draft and had the sick woman drink it. Gradually her writhing lessened and her sobs quieted.

"She'll sleep for a while," he said. "Yumi may give her another dose if the panic returns."

As he spoke the ground shook again. Through the open door Kaede saw the moon quiver as the floor beneath her lifted and subsided. The other maid gave a squeal of fright and ran outside.

"The ground has been shaking all day," Kaede said. "Is it a warning to us of a severe earthquake?"

"Who knows?" Ishida replied. "You had better extinguish the lamps before you go to bed. I'll go home and see what my dog is doing."

"Your dog?"

"If he's asleep under the veranda, there'll be no big quake. But if he's howling, I'll start getting worried."

Ishida chuckled and Kaede realized it had been a long time since she'd seen him in such a good mood. He was a quiet, self-contained, conscientious man guided by his duty to Fujiwara and his calling as a doctor, but she felt something had happened to him that night to penetrate his calm exterior.

He left them, and Yumi followed Kaede into the sleeping room to help her undress.

"The doctor seems cheerful tonight," Kaede remarked. It was so pleasant not to have Rieko listening to her every word that she felt like talking just for the sake of it. The robe slid from her shoulders, and as Yumi lifted her hair to free it, Kaede felt her breath against her ear and heard her whisper.

"That's because Muto Shizuka came to see him."

Kaede felt the blood drain from her head. The room seemed to whirl around her, not from an earth tremor but from her own weakness. Yumi held her to support her and lowered her onto the sleeping mat. She brought out the night robe and helped Kaede put it on.

"My lady must not get cold and fall sick again," she murmured, taking up the comb to attend to Kaede's hair.

"What is the news?" Kaede said quietly.

"The Muto have made a truce with Lord Otori. The Muto master is with him now."

Just hearing his name spoken made Kaede's heart bound so strongly, she thought she would vomit.

"Where is he?"

"At the coast, at Shuho. He surrendered to Lord Arai."

She could not imagine what had been happening to him. "Will he be safe?"

"He and Arai formed an alliance. They will attack Hagi together."

"Another battle," Kaede murmured. A storm of emotion raced through her, making her eyes grow hot. "And my sisters?"

"They are well. A marriage has been arranged for Lady Ai, to Lord Akita's nephew. Please don't cry, lady. No one must ever find out that you know these things. My life depends on it. Shizuka swore to me that you would be able to conceal your feelings."

Kaede fought to keep the tears from falling. "My younger sister?"

"Arai wanted to betroth her to Lord Otori, but he says he will not consider marriage until he has taken Hagi."

It was as if a hidden needle had slipped into her heart. It had not occurred to her, but of course Takeo would marry again. His marriage to her had been annulled; he would be expected to take another wife. Hana was an obvious choice, sealing the alliance with Fujiwara, giving Arai another link to the Maruyama and Shirakawa domains.

"Hana is only a child," she said dully as the comb raked through her hair. Had Takeo forgotten her already? Would he happily accept her sister who looked so much like her? The jealousy that had racked her when she imagined Makoto with him now returned a thousandfold. Her isolation, her imprisonment, struck her with renewed force. *The day I hear he is married I will die, if I have to bite out my own tongue,* she swore silently.

"You may be sure Lord Otori has his own plans," Yumi whispered. "After all, he was riding to rescue you when Arai intercepted him and drove him back to the coast. Only the typhoon prevented his escape then."

"He was coming to rescue me?" Kaede said. The jealousy abated a little, washed away by gratitude and a faint glimmer of hope.

"As soon as he heard of your abduction he set out with over a thousand men." Kaede could feel Yumi trembling. "He sent Shizuka to tell you he loves you and will never give you up. Be patient. He will come for you."

A sound came from the next room, a sort of feverish cry. Both women went still.

"Come with me to the privy," Kaede said, as calmly as if she had said no other words all evening beyond "Hold my robe" and "Comb my hair." She was all too aware of the risks Yumi took by bringing her this message, and feared for her safety.

Yumi took a warm cloak and wrapped it round her. They stepped silently onto the veranda. It was colder than ever.

"It will freeze tonight," the girl remarked. "Shall I order more charcoal for the braziers?"

Kaede listened. The night was still. There was no wind and no dog howling. "Yes, let's try to stay warm."

At the entrance to the privy she slipped the fur robe from her shoulders and gave it to Yumi to hold. Squatting in the dark recess where no one could see her, she let herself feel joy. The words were beating in her brain, the words the goddess herself had spoken to her:

Be patient. He will come for you.

The following day Rieko was a little better; she rose and dressed at her usual time, even though Kaede begged her to rest longer. The autumn wind blew more coldly from the mountain, but Kaede felt a warmth she had not known since her capture. She tried not to think about Takeo, but Yumi's whispered message had brought his image intensely to the forefront of her mind. The words he had sent to her beat so loudly inside her head, she was sure someone would hear them. She was terrified of giving herself away. She did not speak to Yumi or even look at her, but she was aware of a new feeling between them, a kind of complicity. Surely, Rieko with her cormorant eyes could not miss it?

Sickness made Rieko short-tempered and more malicious than ever. She found fault with everything, complained about the food, sent for three different types of tea and found all of them musty, slapped Yumi for not bringing hot water fast enough, and reduced the second maid, Kumiko, to tears when she expressed her fear of earthquakes.

Kumiko was normally lighthearted and cheerful, and Rieko allowed her a certain leeway that the other maids would never have enjoyed. But this morning she sneered at her, laughing in contempt at the girl's fears, ignoring the fact that she herself shared them.

Kaede retreated from the unpleasant atmosphere and went to sit in her favorite place, looking out over the tiny garden. The sun was just barely shining into the room, but in a few weeks it would no longer clear the outer walls. Winter would be gloomy in these rooms—but surely he would come for her before winter?

She could not see the mountains, but she imagined them soaring into the blue autumn sky. They would be snow-capped by now. A bird settled suddenly on the pine tree, chirped loudly, and then flew away again over the roof, a flash of green and white in its wings. It reminded her of the bird Takeo had painted so long ago. Could it be a message for her—a message that she would soon be free?

The women's voices rose behind her. Kumiko was crying: "I can't help it. If the house starts to shake, I have to run outside. I can't bear it."

"So that's what you did last night! You left Her Ladyship on her own, while I was asleep?"

"Yumi was with her all the time," Kumiko answered, weeping.

"Lord Fujiwara's orders were that there must always be two of us with her!" The sound of another slap echoed through the room.

Kaede thought of the bird's flight, the woman's tears. Her own eyes grew hot. She heard footsteps and knew Rieko stood behind her, but she did not turn her head.

"So Lady Fujiwara was alone with Yumi last night. I heard you whispering. What were you talking about?"

"We whispered only so as not to disturb you," Kaede replied. "We spoke of nothing; the autumn wind, the brilliance of the moon, perhaps. I asked her to comb my hair, accompany me to the privy."

Rieko knelt beside her and tried to look into her face. Her heavy scent made Kaede cough.

"Don't bother me," Kaede said, turning away. "We are both unwell. Let us try to spend a peaceful day."

"How ungrateful you are," Rieko said in a voice as tiny as a mosquito's. "And what a fool. Lord Fujiwara has done everything for you and you still dream of deceiving him."

"You must be feverish," Kaede said. "You are imagining things. How could I deceive Lord Fujiwara in any way? I am completely his prisoner."

"His *wife*," Rieko corrected her. "Even to use such a word as *prisoner* shows how you still rebel against your husband."

Kaede said nothing, just gazed at the pine needles etched against the sky. She was afraid of what she might reveal to Rieko. Yumi's message had brought her hope, but the reverse side of hope was fear: for Yumi, for Shizuka, for herself.

"You seem changed in some way," Rieko muttered. "You think I can't read you?"

"It's true I feel a little warm," Kaede said. "I believe the fever has returned."

Are they at Hagi yet? she thought. *Is he fighting now? May he be protected! May he live!*

"I am going to pray for a little while," she told Rieko, and went to kneel before the shrine. Kumiko brought coals and Kaede lit incense. The heavy smell drifted through the rooms, bringing an uneasy peace to the women within.

A few days later Yumi went to fetch the food for the midday meal and did not return. Another maid came in her place, an older woman. She and Kumiko served the meal in silence. Kumiko's eyes were red and she sniffed miserably. When Kaede tried to find out what was wrong, Rieko snapped, "She has caught the cold, that's all."

"Where is Yumi?" Kaede asked.

"You are interested in her? That proves my suspicions were right."

"What suspicions?" Kaede said. "What can you mean? I have no feelings about her one way or the other. I simply wondered where she was."

"You won't be seeing her again," Rieko said coldly. Kumiko made a strangled sound as if she were muffling a sob.

Kaede felt very cold, and yet her skin was burning. She felt as if the walls were closing in on her. By evening her head was aching fiercely; she asked Rieko if she would send for Ishida.

When he came she was appalled at his appearance. A few

days earlier he had been merry; now his face was gaunt and drawn, his eyes like shriveled coals, his skin gray. His manner was as calm as ever and he spoke to her with great kindness, but it was obvious something terrible had happened.

And Rieko knew about it; Kaede was sure of that from her pursed lips and sharp eyes. Not to be able to question the doctor was torture; not to know what was happening in the household around her or in the world outside would surely drive her mad. Ishida gave her tea brewed from willow bark and bade her good night with unusual intensity. She was sure she would never see him again. Despite the sedative, she spent a restless night.

In the morning she questioned Rieko again about Yumi's disappearance and Ishida's distress. When she received no other answer than veiled accusations, she decided she would appeal to Fujiwara himself. It was nearly a week since she had seen him; he had stayed away during their sickness. She could not endure the inexplicably threatening atmosphere any longer.

"Will you tell Lord Fujiwara I would like to see him?" she asked Rieko when she had finished dressing.

The woman went herself and returned to say, "His

Lordship is delighted that his wife desires his company. He has arranged a special entertainment for this evening. He will see you then."

"I would like to speak to him alone," Kaede said.

Rieko shrugged. "There are no special guests at present. Only Mamoru will be with him. You had better bathe, and I suppose we must wash your hair so it can be dried in the sun."

When her hair was at last dry, Rieko insisted on oiling it heavily before she dressed it. Kaede put on the quilted winter robes, grateful for their warmth, for her wet hair had made her very cold, and though the day was sunny, the air was chill. She ate a little soup at midday, but her stomach and throat seemed to have closed against food.

"You are very white," Rieko said. "Lord Fujiwara admires that in a woman." The undertone in her words made Kaede tremble. Something terrible was about to happen—was already happening; everyone knew about it but her, and they would reveal it to her when it pleased them. Her pulse quickened and she felt its rapid thump in her neck, in her belly. From outside came a dull hammering sound that seemed to echo her own heart.

She went to kneel at the shrine, but even that failed to

calm her. At the end of the afternoon Mamoru came and led her to the pavilion where she had watched the first snow fall with Fujiwara at the beginning of the year. Although it was not yet dark, lanterns were already lit in the bare-branched trees, and braziers burned on the veranda. She glanced at the young man, trying to learn something from his demeanor. He was as white as she was, and she thought she detected pity in his eyes. Her alarm deepened.

It had been so long since she had seen any landscape that the scene before her, the gardens and the mountains beyond, seemed unutterably beautiful. The last rays of the sun turned the snowcapped peaks to pink and gold, and the sky was a translucent color between blue and silver. She gazed at it, drinking it in as if it were the last sight she would see on earth.

Mamoru wrapped a bearskin around her and murmured, "Lord Fujiwara will be with you soon."

Directly in front of the veranda was an area of tiny white stones raked into a swirling pattern. Two posts had been newly erected in the center. Kaede frowned at them; they broke the pattern of the stones in a harsh, almost threatening way.

She heard the padding of feet, the rustling of robes.

"His Lordship is approaching," Rieko said behind her, and they both bowed to the ground.

Fujiwara's particular fragrance wafted over Kaede as he sat next to her. He did not speak for a long time, and when he finally told her she might sit up, she thought she heard anger in his voice. Her heart quailed. She tried to call on her courage, but she had none. She was deathly afraid.

"I am glad to see you recovered," he said with icy politeness.

Her mouth was so dry she could hardly speak. "It is thanks to Your Lordship's care," she whispered.

"Rieko said you wished to speak to me."

"I always desire Your Lordship's company," she began, but faltered when his mouth twisted mockingly.

Let me not be afraid, she prayed. *If he sees I am afraid, he will know he has broken me. . . . He is after all only a man; he did not want me to have even a needle. He knows what I can do. He knows I killed Iida.* She drew a deep breath.

"I feel there are things going on that I do not understand. Have I offended Your Lordship? Please tell me what I have done wrong."

"There are things going on that I do not understand,"

he replied. "Almost a conspiracy, I would say. And in my own household. I cannot believe my wife would stoop to such infamy, but Rieko told me of her suspicions and the maid confirmed them before she died."

"What suspicions?" Kaede asked, showing no emotion.

"That someone brought a message to you from Otori."

"Rieko is lying," Kaede said, but her voice did not obey her.

"I don't think so. Your former companion Muto Shizuka was seen in this district. I was surprised. If she wanted to see you, she should have approached me. Then I remembered that Arai had used her as a spy. The maid confirmed that Otori sent her. That was shocking enough, but imagine my astonishment when she was discovered in Ishida's rooms. I was devastated: Ishida, my most trusted servant, almost my friend! How dangerous not to be able to trust one's physician. It would be so easy for him to poison me."

"He is completely trustworthy," Kaede said. "He is devoted to you. Even if it were true that Shizuka brought a message to me from Lord Otori, it has nothing to do with Dr. Ishida."

He looked at her as though she had not grasped what he was saying. "They were sleeping together," he said. "My

223

physician has been having an affair with a woman known to be a spy."

Kaede did not reply. She had not known of their relationship; she had been too wrapped up in her own passion to notice it. Now it seemed quite obvious. She recalled all the signs: how often Shizuka had gone to Ishida's rooms to collect medicine or tea. And now Takeo had sent Shizuka with the message for her. Shizuka and Ishida had risked seeing each other and they were to be punished for it.

The sun had set behind the mountains, but it was not yet dark. Twilight lay over the garden, barely dispelled by the light of the lanterns. A crow flew overhead to its roost, cawing bitterly.

"I am very fond of Ishida," Fujiwara said, "and I know you had become attached to your woman. It's a tragedy, but we must try to comfort each other in our grief." He clapped his hands. "Bring wine, Mamoru. And I think we will begin our entertainment." He leaned toward Kaede. "We don't have to hurry: We have all night."

She still had not grasped his meaning. She glanced at his face, saw the cruel set of his mouth and the skin's pallor, the tiny muscle in his jaw that gave him away. His eyes turned to her and she looked away to the posts. A sudden faintness came over her; the lanterns and the white stones began to swirl around her. She took a deep breath to steady herself.

"Don't do this," she whispered. "It is not worthy of you."

In the distance a dog was howling. It howled and howled without ceasing. *It is Ishida's dog,* Kaede thought, and could almost believe it was her own heart, for it expressed utterly her horror and despair.

"Disobedience and disloyalty to me must be punished," he said, "and in a way that will discourage others."

"If they must die, make it swift," she said. "I will do anything you ask of me in return."

"But you already should do that," he said, almost puzzled. "What else can you offer that a wife should not already do?"

"Be merciful," she begged.

"I do not have a merciful nature," he replied. "You have run out of bargaining power, my dear wife. You thought you could use me for your own purposes. Now I will use you for mine."

Kaede heard footsteps on the gravel. She looked toward the sound as though the power of her gaze could reach

Shizuka and save her. Guards walked slowly to the posts. They were armed with swords and they carried other instruments whose appearance brought a metallic taste of fear to her mouth. Most of the men were somber-faced, but one of them was grinning with nervous excitement. Between them, Ishida and Shizuka were two small figures, weak human bodies with an immense capacity for pain.

Neither of them made a sound as they were tied to the posts, but Shizuka raised her head and looked at Kaede.

This cannot happen. They will take poison, Kaede told herself.

Fujiwara said, "I don't think we left your woman with any way of saving herself, but it will be interesting to see."

Kaede had no idea what Fujiwara intended to do, what torture and cruel death he had devised, but she had heard enough stories at Noguchi Castle to be able to imagine the worst. She realized she was on the edge of losing control. She half rose, in itself unthinkable in Fujiwara's presence, and tried to plead with him, but even as the words came stumbling from her there was a disturbance at the front gate. Guards called out briefly, and two men came into the garden.

One was Murita, the man who had come to escort her and had then ambushed and killed her men. He carried his sword in his left hand; his right hand was still scarred from when she had cut it. She thought she did not know the other, though there was something familiar about him. Both knelt before Fujiwara, and Murita spoke.

"Lord Fujiwara, forgive me for disturbing you, but this man says he brings an urgent message from Lord Arai."

Kaede had sunk to the floor again, grateful for this brief respite. She turned her eyes to the other man, noticed his big hands and long arms, and realized with a shock that it was Kondo. He had dissembled his features, and when he spoke, his voice was changed too. But surely Murita and Fujiwara would know him.

"Lord Fujiwara, Lord Arai sends his greetings to you. Everything is going according to plan."

"Is Otori dead yet?" the nobleman asked, glancing briefly at Kaede.

"Not yet," the man replied. "But in the meantime Lord Arai asks that you return Muto Shizuka to him. He has a particular personal interest in her and wishes to keep her alive."

For a moment Kaede felt hope flood into her heart. Fujiwara would not dare harm Shizuka if Arai wanted her back.

"What a strange request," Fujiwara said, "and a strange messenger." He ordered Murita, "Disarm him. I don't trust him."

The dog howled with a new intensity of fear. It seemed to Kaede that there was a moment of stillness, and then as she tried to call out, as Murita stepped toward Kondo, as Kondo drew his sword, the whole world groaned and lifted. The veranda rose through the air; the trees flew and then crashed; the house behind her shook and was torn apart. More dogs were barking now, frantically. The caged birds shrieked in alarm. The air was full of dust. From the fallen buildings came the screams of women and the instant crackling of fire.

The veranda landed heavily with a thud that shook Kaede's body; the floor was slanting back toward the house, the roof splintering above her. Her eyes were full of fragments of dust and straw. For a moment she thought she was trapped, then she saw that she could climb out and began to scrabble up the strange slope the veranda had assumed. Over its edge she saw as if in a dream Shizuka slip her hands from the bindings, kick one of the guards between the legs, take his sword from him, and slash him in the neck. Kondo had already dealt Murita a blow that had almost cut him in half.

Fujiwara was lying behind Kaede, partly covered by the fallen roof. His body was twisted and he did not seem to be able to get up, but he reached out to her and took her ankle in his hand, the first time he had ever touched her. His fingers were cold and his grip inescapable. The dust was making him cough, his clothes were filthy, and he smelled of sweat and urine beneath the customary fragrance; yet when he spoke his voice was as calm as ever.

"If we are to die, let us die together," he said.

Behind him she could hear the flames, crackling and snarling like a living creature. The smoke thickened, stinging her eyes and masking all the other smells.

She pulled and kicked against his clutching fingers.

"I just wanted to possess you," he said. "You were the most beautiful thing I had ever seen. I wanted you to be mine and no one else's. I wanted to intensify your love for Takeo by denying it so I could share in the tragedy of your suffering."

"Let go of me!" she screamed. She could feel the heat of the fire now. "Shizuka! Kondo! Help me!"

Shizuka was fully occupied with the other guards, fighting like a man. Ishida's hands were still tied to the post.

Kondo killed one of the guards from behind, turned his head at Kaede's voice, and then strode toward the burning house. He leaped onto the edge of the veranda.

"Lady Otori," he said, "I'll free you. Run to the garden, to the pools. Shizuka will look after you." He climbed down and deliberately cut through Fujiwara's wrist. The nobleman gave one harsh scream of pain and outrage; his hand fell from Kaede's ankle.

Kondo pushed her upward and over the edge. "Take my sword. I know you can defend yourself."

He thrust it into her hands and went on swiftly: "I swore allegiance to you. I meant it. I would never let anyone hurt you while I live. But it was a crime for someone like me to kill your father. It's even more of a crime to attack a nobleman and kill him. I'm ready to pay for it."

He gave her a look stripped of all irony and smiled. "Run," he said. "Run! Your husband will come for you."

She stepped backward. She saw Fujiwara try to rise, the blood pouring from the stump of his arm. Kondo wound his long arms round the nobleman and held him firmly. The flames burst through the fragile walls and received them both, wrapping them, concealing them.

The heat and the screams engulfed her. *He is burning, all his treasures are burning,* she thought wildly. She thought she heard Kumiko cry out from the inferno and wanted to do something to save her, but as she started toward the house, Shizuka pulled her back.

"You are on fire!"

Kaede dropped the sword and put her hands uselessly to her head as the flames erupted on her oiled hair.

· 6 ·

The sun set and the moon rose over the still surface of
the sea, making a silver road for our fleet to follow. It
was so bright, I could see clearly the range of mountains
behind the coast we were leaving. The tide rippled under the
hulls and the sails flapped in the offshore breeze. The oars
splashed in a steady rhythm.

We came to Oshima in the early hours of the morning.
A white mist rose from the surface of the sea, and Fumio
told me it would be the same for the next few nights as the
air grew colder. It was perfect for our purpose. We spent the
day on the island, reprovisioning from the pirates' stores and
taking on board more of Terada's men, who were armed with

swords, knives, and a variety of other weapons, most of which I'd never seen before.

At the end of the afternoon we went to the shrine and made offerings to Ebisu and Hachiman, praying for calm seas and the defeat of our enemies. The priests gave us conch shells for each ship and auspicious fortunes that encouraged the men, though Fumio took it all with a certain skepticism, patting his firearm and muttering, "This is more auspicious, in my opinion!" while I was happy enough to pray to any god, knowing that they were simply different faces, created by men, of one indivisible truth.

The moon, one night off full, was rising over the mountains as we set sail for Hagi. This time Kenji, Taku, and I went with Ryoma in his smaller, swifter boat. I left Zenko in Fumio's care, having told him of the boy's parentage and impressing on him the importance of keeping Arai's son alive. Just before dawn the mist began to form above the water, shrouding us as we approached the sleeping city. From across the bay I could hear the first roosters crowing and the early bells from Tokoji and Daishoin.

My plan was to go straight to the castle. I had no desire to destroy my city or see the Otori clan wash blood with blood. I thought that if we could kill or capture the Otori lords right away, there was every chance the clan would side with me rather than tear itself apart. This was also the opinion of the Otori warriors who had already joined me. Many of them had begged to be allowed to accompany me and take part in the vengeance firsthand. They all had experiences of ill treatment, insults, and breaches of faith. But my aim was to penetrate the castle silently and secretly. I would take only Kenji and Taku. I placed all the other men under Terada's command.

The old pirate had been alight with excitement and the anticipation of settling long-standing scores. I'd given him some instructions: The boats were to remain offshore until daybreak. Then they were to sound the conch shells and advance through the mist. The rest was up to him. I hoped to be able to convince the city to surrender; if not, we would fight through the streets to the bridge and open it for Arai's army.

The castle was built on a promontory between the river and the sea. I knew, from my visit on the day of my adoption, that the residence was on the seaward side, where a huge wall, considered to be invulnerable, rose from the water around it.

Kenji and Taku had their grapples and other Tribe weapons. I was armed with throwing knives, a short sword, and Jato.

The moon set and the mist grew thicker. The boat drifted silently toward the shore and nudged the seawall with the faintest of sounds. One by one we climbed onto the wall and went invisible.

I heard footsteps above our heads and a voice called out, "Who's there? Name yourself!"

Ryoma answered in the dialect of a Hagi fisherman, "Only me. Got a bit lost in this dirty mist."

"Got a bit pissed, you mean," a second man called back. "Get out of here! If we can see you when the fog clears, we'll put an arrow in you."

The sound of the oar faded away. I hissed at the other two—I couldn't see either of them—and we began to climb. It was a slow process; the wall, washed twice a day by the tide, was coated in seaweed and slippery. But inch by inch we crawled up it and eventually came to its top. One last autumn cricket was chirping and it fell suddenly silent. Kenji chirped in its place. I could hear the guards talking at the far corner of the bailey. A lamp and a brazier burned beside them.

Beyond them lay the residence where the Otori lords, their retainers, and families would be sleeping.

I could hear only two voices, which surprised me. I'd thought there would be more, but from their conversation I gathered that all available men had been posted on the bridge and along the river in anticipation of Arai's attack.

"Wish he'd get it over with," one of them grumbled. "It's this waiting I can't stand."

"He must know how little food there is in the town," the other replied. "Probably thinks he can starve us out."

"I suppose it's better to have him out there than in here."

"Enjoy it while you can. If the town falls to Arai, it'll be a bloodbath. Even Takeo ran away into a typhoon rather than face Arai!"

I felt alongside me for Taku, found his shape, and pulled his head close to me. "Go inside the wall," I mouthed in his ear. "Distract them while we take them from behind."

I felt him nod and heard the tiny sound as he moved away. Kenji and I followed him over the wall. In the glow from the brazier I suddenly caught sight of a small shadow. It flitted across the ground and then divided in two, silent and ghostly.

"What was that?" one of the guards exclaimed.

They were both on their feet and staring toward Taku's two images. It was easy for us: We took one each, soundlessly.

The guards had just made tea, so we drank it while we waited for daybreak. The sky paled gradually. There was no separation between it and the water; it was all one shimmering surface. When the conch shells began to sound, the hair stood up on the back of my neck. Dogs howled in response from the shore.

I heard the household within erupt into activity: the padding of feet, not yet frantic, cries of surprise, not yet alarm. The shutters were thrown open, and the doors slid apart. A group of guards rushed out, followed by Shoichi and Masahiro, still in night attire but with their swords in their hands.

They stopped dead as I walked toward them, Jato unsheathed in my hand, the mist wreathing around me. Behind me the first ships were appearing; the conch shells sang again over the water and the sound echoed back from the mountains around the bay.

Masahiro took a step back. "Shigeru?" he gasped.

His older brother went white. They saw the man they

had tried to murder; they saw the Otori sword in his hand, and they were terrified.

I said in a loud voice, "I am Otori Takeo, grandson of Shigemori, nephew and adopted son of Shigeru. I hold you responsible for the death of the rightful heir to the Otori clan. You sent Shintaro to assassinate him, and when that failed, you conspired with Iida Sadamu to murder him. Iida has already paid with his life, and now you will!"

I was aware that Kenji stood behind me, sword drawn, and hoped Taku was still invisible. I did not take my eyes off the men in front of me.

Shoichi tried to regain his composure. "Your adoption was illegal. You have no claim to Otori blood nor to the sword you carry. We do not recognize you." He called to the retainers. "Cut them down!"

Jato seemed to quiver in my hands as it came alive. I was prepared to meet the attack, but no one moved. I saw Shoichi's face change as he realized he was going to have to fight me himself.

"I have no wish to split the clan," I said. "My only desire is for your heads." I thought I'd given them enough warning. I could feel Jato thirsting for blood. It was as though

Shigeru's spirit had taken me over and would have his revenge.

Shoichi was the closer and I knew he was the better swordsman. I would get rid of him first. They had both been good fighters, but they were now old men in their late forties and they wore no armor. I was at the height of speed and fitness, flesh and bone planed by hardship and war. I killed Shoichi with a blow to the neck that cut him diagonally. Masahiro swung at me from behind, but Kenji parried the stroke, and as I spun to meet my other opponent I saw fear distort his face. I pushed him back toward the wall. He avoided each stroke, weaving and parrying, but his heart was not in it. He made one last appeal to his men, but still not one of them moved.

The first ships were not far offshore. Masahiro looked behind him, looked back, and saw Jato descend on him. He made a frantic, ducking movement and fell over the wall.

Furious that he had escaped me, I was about to jump after him when his son, Yoshitomi, my old enemy from the fighting hall, came running from the residence, followed by a handful of his brothers and cousins. None of them was more than twenty.

"I'll fight you, sorcerer," Yoshitomi cried. "Let's see if you can fight like a warrior!"

I had gone into an almost supernatural state, and Jato was enraged by now and had tasted blood. It moved faster than the eye could follow. Whenever I seemed to be out-numbered, Kenji was at my side. I was sorry such young men had to die but glad that they, too, paid for the treachery of their fathers. When I was able to turn my attention back to Masahiro, I saw he had surfaced near a small boat at the front of the line of ships. It was Ryoma's. Seizing his father by his hair, the young man pulled him upward and cut his throat with one of the knives fishermen use to gut fish. Whatever Masahiro's crimes, this was a far more terrible death than any I could have devised for him: to be killed by his own son while trying to escape in fear.

I turned to face the crowd of retainers. "I have a huge force of men on the ships out there and Lord Arai is in alliance with me. I have no quarrel with any of you. You may take your own lives, you may serve me, or you may fight me one-on-one now. I have fulfilled my duty to Lord Shigeru and done what he commanded."

I could still feel his spirit inhabiting me.

One of the older men stepped forward. I remembered his face, but his name escaped me.

"I am Endo Chikara. Many of us have sons and nephews who have already joined you. We have no desire to fight our own children. You have done what was your duty and your right in a fair and honorable way. For the sake of the clan, I am prepared to serve you, Lord Otori."

With that he knelt and one by one the others followed. Kenji and I went through the residence and placed guards on the women and children. I hoped the women would take their own lives honorably. I would decide what to do with the children later. We checked all the secret places and flushed out several spies hidden there. Some were obviously Kikuta, but neither in the residence nor the castle was there any sign of Kotaro, who Kenji had been told was in Hagi.

Endo came with me to the castle. The captain of the guard there was equally relieved to be able to surrender to me; his name was Miyoshi Satoru: He was Kahei and Gemba's father. Once the castle was secured, the boats came to shore and the men disembarked to move through the town street by street.

Taking the castle, which I had thought would be the

hardest part of my plan, turned out to be the easiest. Despite its surrender and my best efforts, the town did not give in altogether peacefully. The streets were in chaos; people tried to flee, but there was nowhere to go. Terada and his men had scores of their own to settle, and there were pockets of stubborn resistance that we had to overcome in fierce hand-to-hand fighting.

Finally we came to the banks of the western river, not far from the stone bridge. Judging by the sun, it must have been late afternoon. The mist had lifted long ago, but smoke from burning houses hung above the river. On the opposite bank, the last of the maple leaves were brilliant red and the willows along the water's edge were yellow. The leaves were falling, drifting in the eddies. Late chrysanthemums bloomed in gardens. In the distance I could see the fish weir, and the tiled walls along the bank.

My house is there, I thought. *I will sleep there tonight.*

But the river was full of men swimming and small boats loaded to the gunwales, while a long stream of soldiers pressed toward the bridge.

Kenji and Taku were still alongside me, Taku silenced by what he had seen of war. We stared at the sight: the remnants of the Otori army in defeat. I was filled with pity for them and anger at their lords who had so misled and betrayed them, leaving them to fight this desperate rearguard action while they slept comfortably in Hagi Castle.

I had been separated from Fumio, but now I saw him at the bridge with a handful of his men. They seemed to be arguing with a group of Otori captains. We went over to them. Zenko was with Fumio, and he smiled briefly at his brother. They stood close to each other but did not say anything.

"This is Lord Otori Takeo," Fumio told the men when I approached. "The castle has surrendered to him. He'll tell you." He turned to me. "They want to destroy the bridge and prepare for siege. They don't believe in the alliance with Arai. They've been fighting him off for the last week. He's right behind them. They say their only hope is to get the bridge down immediately."

I removed my helmet so they could see my face. They immediately dropped to their knees. "Arai has sworn to support me," I said. "The alliance is genuine. Once he knows the town has surrendered, he will cease the attack."

"Let's break the bridge down anyway," their leader said.

I thought of the ghost of the stonemason entombed

alive in his creation and of the inscription that Shigeru had read aloud to me: *The Otori clan welcome the just and the loyal. Let the unjust and the disloyal beware.* I did not want to destroy such a precious thing, and anyway, I could not see how they would dismantle it in time.

"No, let it stand," I replied. "I will answer for Lord Arai's faithfulness. Tell your men they have nothing to fear if they surrender to me and accept me as their lord."

Endo and Miyoshi came up on horseback and I sent them to carry the message to the Otori soldiers. Little by little the confusion settled. We cleared the bridge and Endo rode to the other side to organize a more orderly return to the town. Many men were reassured enough to settle down where they were and rest, while others decided they might as well go home, and set off for their farms and houses.

Miyoshi said, "You should be on horseback, Lord Takeo," and gave me his horse, a good-looking black that reminded me of Aoi. I mounted, rode across the bridge to speak to the men there, causing them to break out into cheers, and then rode back with Endo. When the cheers died away I could hear the distant sound of Arai's army approaching, the tramping of horses and men.

They came down the valley, a stream of ants in the distance, Kumamoto and Seishuu banners unfurled. As they came closer I recognized Arai at their head: chestnut horse, stag-antlered helmet, red-laced armor.

I leaned down to say to Kenji, "I should go and meet him."

Kenji frowned as he peered across the river. "Something feels wrong," he said quietly.

"What?"

"I don't know. Be on your guard and don't cross the bridge."

As I urged the black forward slightly, Endo said, "I am the senior retainer of the Otori clan. Let me take news of our surrender to you to Lord Arai."

"Very well," I said. "Tell him to encamp his army on that side of the river and bring him into the town. Then we can enforce peace with no further bloodshed on either side."

Endo rode forward onto the bridge and Arai halted and waited on the other side. Endo was almost halfway across when Arai held up his hand with the black war fan in it.

There was a moment of silence. Zenko cried at my side, "They are arming their bows."

The war fan dropped.

Though it was happening right in front of my eyes, I could not believe it. For several moments I stared incredulous as the arrows began to fall. Endo went down at once, and the men on the bank, unarmed and unprepared, fell like deer to the hunter.

"There," Kenji said, drawing his sword. "That's what's wrong."

Once before I had been so betrayed—but that had been by Kenji himself and the Tribe. This betrayal was by a warrior to whom I had sworn allegiance. Had I killed Jo-An for this? Fury and outrage turned my vision red. I had taken the impregnable castle, kept the bridge whole, pacified the men. I had handed Hagi, my town, to Arai like a ripe persimmon, and with it the Three Countries.

Dogs were howling in the distance. They sounded like my own soul.

Arai rode onto the bridge and came to a halt in the center. He saw me and lifted off his helmet. It was a derisive gesture. He was so sure of his own strength, of victory. "Thank you, Otori," he called. "What a good work you did. Will you surrender now or shall we fight it out?"

"You may rule over the Three Countries," I shouted back,

"but your falsehood will be remembered long after your death." I knew I was about to fight my last battle, and it was, as I had known it must be, with Arai. I just had not realized it would come so quickly.

"There will be no one left to record it," he sneered in reply, "because I intend now to wipe out the Otori once and for all."

I leaned down and seized Zenko, pulling him up onto the horse in front of me. I took my short sword and held it to his neck.

"I have both your sons here. Will you condemn them to death? I swear to you, I will kill Zenko now and Taku after him before you can reach me. Call off your attack!"

His face changed a little and paled. Taku stood motionless next to Kenji. Zenko did not move, either. Both boys stared at the father they had not seen for years.

Then Arai's features hardened and he laughed. "I know you, Takeo. I know your weakness. You were not raised as a warrior; let's see if you can bring yourself to kill a child."

I should have acted immediately and ruthlessly, but I did not. I hesitated. Arai laughed again.

"Let him go," he called. "Zenko! Come here to me."

Fumio called in a low, clear voice, "Takeo, shall I shoot him?"

I can't remember replying. I can't remember letting go of Zenko. I heard the muffled report from the firearm and saw Arai recoil in the saddle as the ball hit him, piercing his armor above the heart. There was a cry, of rage and horror, from the men around him and a scuffle as his horse reared; Zenko screamed, but these sounds were as nothing to the roar that followed them as the world beneath my horse's feet tore itself apart.

The maples on the far shore rose almost gracefully and began to march down the hillside. They gathered up Arai's army as they went, wrapping them in stones and soil and rolling them into the river.

My horse backed in terror, reared, and fled from the bridge, throwing me sideways onto the road. As I got to my feet, winded, the bridge groaned with a human voice. It cried out in its efforts to hold itself together and then flew apart, taking everyone on it down into the river. Then the river itself went mad. From the confluence upstream came a yellow-brown flood of water. It drained away from the bank on the town side, gathering up boats and living beings impartially, and raced over the opposite bank, where it swept away the remnants of two armies, breaking the boats like eating sticks, drowning men and horses and carrying their corpses out to sea.

The ground shook fiercely again, and from behind me I heard the crash of collapsing houses. I felt as if I'd been stunned: Everything around me was hazy with dust and muffled so I could no longer hear distinct sounds. I was aware of Kenji beside me and Taku kneeling by his brother, who had also fallen when the horse reared. I saw Fumio coming toward me through the haze, the firearm still in his hand.

I was shaking from some mixture of emotions close to elation: a recognition of how puny we humans are when confronted with the great forces of nature, combined with gratitude to heaven, to the gods I'd thought I did not believe in, who once again had spared my life.

My last battle had begun and ended in a moment. There was no further thought of fighting. Our only concern now was to save the town from fire.

Much of the district around the castle burned to the ground. The castle itself was destroyed in one of the aftershocks, killing the remaining women and children who were being held there. I was relieved, for I knew I could not let them live, but I shrank from ordering their deaths. Ryoma also died then, his boat sunk by falling masonry. When his body was washed up days later, I had him buried with the Otori lords at Daishoin, their name on his gravestone.

In the next few days I hardly slept or ate. With Miyoshi and Kenji's help I organized the survivors to clear the rubble, bury the dead, and care for the wounded. Through the long sorrowful days of work and cooperation and grief, the rifts in the clan began to heal. The earthquake was generally held to be heaven's punishment on Arai for his treachery. Heaven clearly favored me, I was Shigeru's adopted son and nephew by blood, I had his sword, I resembled him, and I had avenged his death: The clan accepted me unreservedly as his true heir. I did not know what the situation was in the rest of the land; the earthquakes had shattered much of the Three Countries and we heard nothing from the other cities. All I was aware of was the enormity of the task that faced me in restoring peace and preventing famine in the coming winter.

I did not sleep at Shigeru's house the night of the earthquake, nor for many days following. I could not bear to go near it in case it had been destroyed. I camped with Miyoshi in what remained of his residence. But about four days after the earthquake, Kenji came to me one evening after I had eaten and told me there was someone to see me. He was grinning, and for a moment I imagined it might be Shizuka with a message from Kaede.

Instead it was the maids from Shigeru's house, Chiyo and Haruka. They looked exhausted and frail, and when they saw me I was afraid Chiyo would die from emotion. They both knelt at my feet, but I made them get up and I embraced Chiyo as tears streamed down her face. None of us could speak.

Finally, Chiyo said, "Come home, Lord Takeo. The house is waiting for you."

"It's still standing?"

"The garden is ruined—the river swept through it—but the house is not badly damaged. We'll get it ready for you tomorrow."

"I will come tomorrow evening," I promised.

"You will come, too, sir?" she said to Kenji.

"Almost like old times," he replied, smiling, though we all knew it could never be that.

The following day Kenji and I took Taku and some guards and walked down the familiar street. I did not take Zenko. The circumstances surrounding Arai's death had left his older son deeply disturbed. I was concerned for him, seeing his confusion and grief, but did not have time to deal with it. I suspected that he thought his father had died ignobly and blamed me for it. Maybe he even blamed or despised me for sparing his life. I myself was not sure how to treat him: as the heir to a mighty warlord or as the son of the man who had betrayed me. I thought it best for him to be kept out of my way for the time being and put him in the service of Endo Chikara's family. I still hoped his mother, Shizuka, was alive; when she returned we would discuss her son's future. Taku I had no doubts about; I would keep him with me, the first of the child spies I had dreamed of training and employing.

The district around my old house had been hardly touched by the earthquake, and birds were singing blithely in the gardens. As we walked through it I was thinking about how I used to wait for the exact moment when I heard the house's song of the river and the world, and remembering how I had first seen Kenji on the corner. The song was altered now; the stream was clogged, the waterfall dry, but the river still lapped at the dock and the wall.

Haruka found the last of the wildflowers and a few chrysanthemums to put in buckets outside the kitchen, as she always had, and their sharp autumn scent mingled with the smell of mud and decay from the river. The garden was ruined, the fish all dead, but Chiyo had washed and polished the nightingale floor, and when we stepped onto it, it sang beneath our feet.

The downstairs rooms were damaged by water and mud, and she had already started stripping them and having new mats laid, but the upstairs room was untouched. She had cleaned and polished it until it looked just as it had the first time I had seen it when I had fallen in love with Shigeru's house and with him.

Chiyo apologized that there was no hot water for a bath, but we washed in cold water and she managed to find enough food for an adequate meal as well as several flasks of wine. We ate in the upper room, as we so often had before, and Kenji made Taku laugh by describing my poor efforts as a student and how impossible and disobedient I had been. I was filled with an almost unbearable mixture of sorrow and joy, and smiled with tears in my eyes. But whatever my grief, I felt Shigeru's spirit was at peace. I could almost see his quiet ghost in the room with us, smiling when we smiled. His murderers were dead and Jato had come home.

Taku fell asleep at last, and Kenji and I shared one more flask of wine as we watched the gibbous moon move across the garden. It was a cold night. There would probably be a frost, and we closed the shutters before going to bed ourselves. I slept restlessly, no doubt from the wine, and woke just before dawn, thinking I had heard some unfamiliar sound.

The house lay quiet around me. I could hear Kenji and Taku breathing alongside me, and Chiyo and Haruka in the room below. We had put guards on the gate, and there were still a couple of dogs there. I thought I could hear the guards talking in low voices. Perhaps it was they who had awakened me.

I lay and listened for a while. The room began to lighten as day broke. I decided I had heard nothing unusual and would go to the privy before I tried to sleep for another hour or two. I got up quietly and crept down the stairs, slid open the door, and stepped outside.

I did not bother masking my footsteps, but as soon as

the floor sang I realized what it was I had heard: one light step onto the boards. Someone had tried to come into the house and had been discouraged by the floor. So where was he now?

I was thinking rapidly, *I should wake Kenji, should at least get a weapon,* when the Kikuta master Kotaro came out of the misty garden and stood in front of me.

Until tonight I had seen him only in his faded blue robes, the disguise he wore when traveling. Now he was in the dark fighting clothes of the Tribe, and all the power that he usually kept hidden was revealed in his stance and in his face, the embodiment of the Tribe's hostility toward me, expert, ruthless, and implacable.

He said, "I believe your life is forfeit to me."

"You broke faith with me by ordering Akio to kill me," I said. "All our bargains were annulled then. And you had no right to demand anything from me when you did not tell me that it was you who killed my father."

He smiled in contempt. "You're right, I did kill Isamu," he said. "I've learned now what it was that made him disobedient too: the Otori blood that flows in you both." He reached into his jacket and I moved quickly to avoid the knife I thought was

255

coming, but what he held out was a small stick. "I drew this," he said, "and I obeyed the orders of the Tribe, even though Isamu and I were cousins and friends, and even though he refused to defend himself. That's what obedience is."

Kotaro's eyes were fixed on my face and I knew he was hoping to confuse me with the Kikuta sleep, but I was certain I could withstand it, though I doubted I could use it on him as I had once before in Matsue. We held each other's gaze for several moments, neither of us able to dominate.

"You murdered him," I said. "You contributed to Shigeru's death too. And what purpose did Yuki's death serve?"

He hissed impatiently in the way I remembered and with a lightning movement threw the stick to the ground and drew a knife. I dove sideways, shouting loudly. I had no illusions about my ability to take him on alone and unarmed. I would have to fight bare-handed as I had with Akio until someone came to my help.

He jumped after me, feinting at me, and then moved faster than the eye could follow in the opposite direction to take my neck in a stranglehold; but I'd anticipated the move, slipped under his grasp, and kicked at him from behind. I caught him just over the kidney and heard him grunt. Then

I leaped above him and with my right hand hit him in the neck.

The knife came upward and I felt it slash deep into the side of my right hand, taking off the two smallest fingers and opening up the palm. It was my first real wound and the pain was terrible, worse than anything I'd ever experienced. I went invisible for a moment, but my blood betrayed me, spurting across the nightingale floor. I shouted again, screaming for Kenji, for the guards, and split myself. The second self rolled across the floor while I drove my left hand into Kotaro's eyes.

His head snapped sideways as he avoided the blow, and I kicked at the hand that held the knife. He leaped away with unbelievable speed and then seemed to fly back at my head. I ducked just before he could kick me in the head and leaped into the air as he landed, all this time fighting off shock and pain, knowing that if I gave in to them for a moment, I would die. I was about to try to kick him in a similar way when I heard the upstairs window open and a small invisible object came hurtling out.

Kotaro was not expecting it and he heard it a second after I did. By then I had perceived it to be Taku. I leaped to break his fall, but he seemed almost to fly down onto

Kotaro, distracting him momentarily. I turned my leap into a kick and rammed my foot hard into Kotaro's neck.

As I landed, Kenji shouted from above, "Takeo! Here!" and threw Jato down to me.

I caught my sword in my left hand. Kotaro grabbed Taku, swung him above his head, and hurled him into the garden. I heard the boy gasp as he landed. I swung Jato above my head, but my right hand was pouring blood and the blade descended crookedly. Kotaro went invisible as I missed him. But now that I was armed he was more wary of me. I had a moment's breathing space. I tore off my sash and wound it around my palm.

Kenji leaped from the upstairs window, landed on his feet like a cat, and immediately went invisible. I could discern the two masters faintly and they could obviously see each other. I had fought alongside Kenji before and I knew if anyone did how truly dangerous he was, but I realized I had never seen him in action against anyone who had a fraction of his skills. He had a sword a little longer than Kotaro's knife and it gave him a slight advantage, but Kotaro was both brilliant and desperate. They drove each other up and down the floor and it cried out under their feet. Kotaro seemed to stumble, but as Kenji closed in on him, he recovered and kicked him in the ribs. They both split their images. I lunged at Kotaro's second self as Kenji somersaulted away from him. Kotaro turned to deal with me and I heard the whistling sound of throwing knives. Kenji had hurled them at his neck. The first blade penetrated and I saw Kotaro's vision begin to waver. His eyes were fixed on my face. He made one last vain thrust with his knife, but Jato seemed to anticipate it and found its way into his throat. He tried to curse me as he died, but his windpipe was slashed and only blood came bubbling out, obscuring the words.

By now the sun had risen; when we gazed down on Kotaro's broken, bleeding body in its pale light, it was hard to believe that such a fragile human being had wielded so much power. Kenji and I had only just managed to overcome him between us and he had left me with a ruined hand, Kenji with terrible bruises and, we found out later, broken ribs. Taku was winded and shaken, lucky to be still alive. The guards who had come running at my shouts were as shocked as if a demon had attacked us. The dogs' hackles rose when they sniffed around the body, and they showed their teeth in uneasy snarls.

My fingers were gone, my palm was torn open. Once the terror and thrill of the fight had subsided, the pain truly made itself felt, turning me faint.

Kenji said, "The knife blade was probably poisoned. We should take your hand off at the elbow to save your life." I was light-headed with shock and at first thought he was joking, but his face was serious and his voice alarmed me. I made him promise he would not do it. I would rather be dead than lose what was left of my right hand. As it was, I thought I would never hold a sword or a brush again.

He washed the wound at once, told Chiyo to bring coals, and, while the guards knelt on me to hold me still, seared the stumps of the fingers and the edges of the wound and then bound it with what he said he hoped was an antidote.

The blade was indeed poisoned and I fell into hell, a confusion of pain and fever and despair. As the long, tormented days passed, I was aware that everyone thought I was dying. I did not believe I would die, but I could not speak to reassure the living. Instead, I lay in the upstairs room, thrashing and sweating and babbling to the dead.

They filed past me, those I had killed, those who had died for me, those I had avenged: my family in Mino; the Hidden at Yamagata; Shigeru; Ichiro; the men I had murdered on the Tribe's orders; Yuki; Amano; Jiro; Jo-An.

I longed for them to be alive again, I longed to see them in the flesh and hear their living voices; one by one they bade me farewell and left me, desolate and alone. I wanted to follow them, but I could not find the road they had taken.

At the worst point of the fever, I opened my eyes and saw a man in the room. I had never seen him before, but I knew he was my father. He wore peasant's clothes like the men of my village and he carried no weapons. The walls faded away and I was in Mino again; the village was unburned and the rice fields were brilliant green. I watched my father working in the fields, absorbed and peaceful. I followed him up the mountain path and into the forest and I knew how much he loved to roam there among its animals and plants, for it was what I loved too.

I saw him turn his head and listen in the familiar Kikuta way as he caught some distant noise. In a moment he would recognize the step: his cousin and friend who was coming to execute him. I saw Kotaro appear on the path in front of him.

He was dressed in the dark fighting clothes of the Tribe, as he had been when he came for me. The two men stood as if frozen before me, each with their distinctive stance: my father, who had taken a vow never to kill again, and the future Kikuta master, who lived by the trade of death and terror.

As Kotaro drew his knife I screamed out a warning. I tried to rise, but hands held me back. The vision faded, leaving me in anguish. I knew that I could not change the past, but I was aware, with the intensity of fever, that the conflict was still unresolved. However much men craved an end to violence, it seemed they could not escape it. It would go on and on forever unless I found a middle way, a way to bring peace, and the only way I could think of was to reserve all violence to myself, in the name of my country and my people. I would have to continue on my violent path so that everyone else could live free of it, just as I had to believe in nothing so everyone else was free to believe in what they wanted. I did not want that. I wanted to follow my father and forswear killing, living in the way my mother had taught me. The darkness rose around me and I knew that if I surrendered to it I could go after him and the conflict would be ended for me. The thinnest of veils separated me from the next world, but a voice was echoing through the shadows.

Your life is not your own. Peace comes at the price of bloodshed.

Behind the holy woman's words I heard Makoto calling my name. I did not know if he was dead or alive. I wanted to explain to him what I had learned and how I could not bear to act as I knew I would have to and so I was leaving with my father, but when I tried to speak, my swollen tongue would not frame the words. They came out as nonsense and I writhed in frustration, thinking we would be parted before I could talk to him.

He was holding my hands firmly. He leaned close and spoke clearly to me. "Takeo! I know. I understand. It's all right. We will have peace. But only you can bring it. You must not die. Stay with us! You have to stay with us for the sake of peace."

He talked to me like this for the rest of the night, his voice keeping the ghosts at bay and linking my spirit with this world. Dawn came and the fever broke. I slept deeply, and when I awoke, lucidity had returned. Makoto was still there and I wept for joy that he was alive. My hand still throbbed, but with the ordinary pain of healing, not with the ferocious agony of the poison. Kenji told me later he thought something must have come from my father, some immunity in the master poisoner's blood that protected me. It was then that I repeated to him the words of the prophecy, how my own son was destined to kill me and how I did not believe I would die before then. He was silent for a long time.

"Well," he said finally. "That must lie a long way in the future. We will deal with it when it comes."

My son was Kenji's grandson. The prophecy seemed even more unbearably cruel to me. I was still weak and tears came easily. My body's frailty infuriated me. It was seven days before I could walk outside to the privy, fifteen before I could get on a horse again. The full moon of the eleventh month came and went. Soon it would be the solstice and then the year would turn, the snows would come. My hand began to heal: The wide, ugly scar almost obliterated both the silvery mark, from the burn I received the day Shigeru saved my life, and the straight line of the Kikuta.

Makoto sat with me day and night but said little to me. I felt he was keeping something from me and that Kenji also knew what it was. Once they brought Hiroshi to see me and I was relieved that the boy lived. He seemed cheerful, telling me about their journey, how they had escaped the worst of the earthquake and had come upon the pathetic remnants of Arai's once mighty army, and how marvelous Shun had been, but I thought he was partly pretending. Sometimes Taku, who had aged years in a month, came to sit by me; like Hiroshi, he acted cheerfully, but his face was pale and strained. As my strength returned, I realized we should have heard from Shizuka. Obviously everyone feared the worst, but I did not believe she was dead. Nor was Kaede, for neither of them had visited me in my delirium.

Finally one evening Makoto said to me, "We have had news from the South. The damage from the earthquake was even more severe there. At Lord Fujiwara's there was a terrible fire. . . ."

He took my hand. "I'm sorry, Takeo. It seems no one survived."

"Fujiwara is dead?"

"Yes, his death is confirmed." He paused and added quietly, "Kondo Kiichi died there."

Kondo, whom I had sent with Shizuka . . .

"And your friend?" I asked.

"He also. Poor Mamoru. I think he would almost have welcomed it."

I said nothing for a few moments. Makoto said gently, "They have not found her body, but . . ."

"I must know for sure," I said. "Will you go there for me?"

He agreed to leave the next morning. I spent the night anguishing over what I would do if Kaede was dead. My only desire would be to follow her; yet how could I desert all those who had stayed so loyally by me? By dawn I'd recognized the truth of Jo-An's words, and Makoto's. My life was not my own. Only I could bring peace. I was condemned to live.

During the night something else occurred to me, and I asked to see Makoto before he left. I was worried about the records that Kaede had taken to Shirakawa with her. If I was to live, I wanted to have them back in my possession before winter began. For I had to spend the long months in planning the summer's strategy; those of my enemies who remained would not hesitate to use the Tribe against me. I felt I would have to leave Hagi in the spring and impose my rule over the Three Countries, maybe even set up my headquarters in Inuyama and make it my capital. It made me smile half-bitterly, for its name means Dog Mountain, and it was as if it had been waiting for me.

I told Makoto to take Hiroshi with him. The boy would show him where the records were hidden. I could not suppress the fluttering hope that Kaede would be at Shirakawa—that Makoto would somehow bring her back to me.

They returned on a bitterly cold day nearly two weeks later. I saw they were alone, and disappointment nearly overcame me. They were also empty-handed.

"The old woman who guards the shrine would give the records to no one but you," Makoto said. "I'm sorry, I could not persuade her otherwise."

Hiroshi said eagerly, "We will go back. I will go with Lord Otori."

"Yes, Lord Otori must go," Makoto said. He seemed to be going to speak again but then fell silent.

"What?" I prompted him.

He was looking at me with a strange expression of compassion and pure affection. "We will all go," he said. "We will learn once and for all if there is any news of Lady Otori."

I longed to go yet feared it would be a useless journey and that it was too late in the year. "We run the risk of being caught by the snow," I said. "I had planned to winter in Hagi."

"If the worse comes to the worst, you can stay in Terayama. I am going there on the way back. I will be staying there, for I can see my time with you is drawing to a close."

"You are going to leave me? Why?"

"I feel I have other work to do. You have achieved all that I set out to help you with. I am being called back to the temple."

I was devastated. Was I to lose everyone I loved? I turned away to hide my feelings.

"When I thought you were dying, I made a vow," Makoto went on. "I promised the Enlightened One that if you lived, I would devote my life to your cause in a different way. I've fought and killed alongside you and I would do it gladly all over again. Except that it solves nothing, in the end. Like the weasel's dance, the cycle of violence goes on and on."

His words rang in my ears. They were exactly what had pounded in my brain while I was delirious.

"You talked in your fever about your father and about the command of the Hidden, to take no one's life. As a warrior, it's hard for me to understand, but as a monk it is a command that I feel I must try and follow. I vowed that night that I would never kill again. Instead, I will seek peace through prayer and meditation. I left my flutes at Terayama to take up weapons. I will leave my weapons here and go back for them."

He smiled slightly. "When I speak the words, they sound like madness. I am taking the first step only on a long and difficult journey, but it is one I must make."

I said nothing in reply. I pictured the temple at Terayama where Shigeru and Takeshi were buried, where I had been sheltered and nurtured, where Kaede and I had been married. It lay in the center of the Three Countries, the physical and spiritual heart of my land and my life. And from now on Makoto would be there, praying for the peace I longed for, always upholding my cause. He would be one person, like a tiny splash of dye in a huge vat, but I could see the color spreading over the years, the blue-green color that the word *peace* always summoned up for me. Under Makoto's influence the temple would become a place of peace, as its founder had intended it to be.

"I am not leaving you," he said gently. "I will be with you in a different way."

I had no words to express my gratitude: He had understood my conflict completely and in this way was taking the first steps to resolve it. All I could do was thank him and let him go.

Kenji, supported tacitly by Chiyo, argued strongly against my decision to travel, saying I was asking for trouble by undertaking such a journey before I was fully recovered. I felt better every day and my hand had mostly healed, though it still pained me and I still felt my phantom fingers. I grieved for the loss of all my dexterity and tried to accustom my left hand to the sword and the brush, but at least I held a horse's reins in that hand and I thought I was well enough to ride. My main concern was that I was needed in the reconstruction of Hagi, but Miyoshi Kahei and his father assured me they could manage without me. Kahei and the rest of my army had been delayed with Makoto by the earthquake but were unharmed by it. Their arrival had greatly increased our forces and hastened the town's recovery. I told Kahei to send messages as soon as possible to Shuho, to invite the master carpenter Shiro and his family back to the clan.

In the end Kenji gave in and said, despite the considerable pain of his broken ribs, he would of course accompany me, since I'd shown myself unable to deal with Kotaro alone. I forgave him his sarcasm, glad to have him with me, and we took Taku as well, not wanting to leave him behind while he was so low in spirits. He and Hiroshi squabbled as usual, but Hiroshi had grown more patient and Taku less arrogant and I could see a true friendship was developing between them. I also took as many men as we could spare from the town and left them in groups along the road to help rebuild the stricken villages and farms. The earthquake had cut a swath from north to south and we followed its line. It was close to midwinter; despite the loss and destruction, people were getting ready for the New Year's celebration; their lives were starting again.

The days were frosty but clear; the landscape bare and wintering. Snipe called from the marshes, and the colors were gray and muted. We rode directly south and in the evenings the sun sank red in the West, the only color in a dulled world. The nights were intensely cold with huge stars, and every morning was white with frost.

I knew Makoto was keeping some secret from me, but could not tell if it was to be a happy one or not. Every day he seemed to shine more with some inner anticipation. My own spirits were still volatile. I was pleased to be riding Shun again, but the cold and the hardship of the journey, together with the pain and disability in my hand, were more draining than I had thought they would be, and at night the task in front of me seemed too immense for me ever to achieve, especially if I was to attempt it without Kaede.

On the seventh day we came to Shirakawa. The sky had clouded over and the whole world seemed gray. Kaede's home was in ruins and deserted. The house had burned and there was nothing left of it but charred beams and ashes. It looked unutterably mournful; I imagined Fujiwara's residence would look the same. I had a serious premonition that she was dead and that Makoto was taking me to her grave. A shrike scolded us from the burned trunk of a tree by the gate, and in the rice fields two crested ibis were feeding, their pink plumage glowing in the forlorn landscape. However, as we rode away past the water meadows Hiroshi called to me: "Lord Otori! Look!"

Two brown mares were trotting toward us, whinnying to our horses. They both had foals at foot, three months old, I reckoned, their brown baby hair just beginning to give way to gray. They had manes and tails as black as lacquer.

"They are Raku's colts!" Hiroshi said. "Amano told me that the Shirakawa mares were in foal to him."

I could not stop looking at them. They seemed like an

inexpressibly precious gift from heaven, from life itself, a promise of renewal and rebirth.

"One of them will be yours," I said to Hiroshi. "You deserve it for your loyalty to me."

"Can the other one go to Taku?" Hiroshi begged.

"Of course!"

The boys yelped with delight. I told the grooms to bring the mares with us, and the foals gamboled after them, cheering me enormously as we followed Hiroshi's lead, riding along the Shirakawa to the sacred caves.

I had never been there before and was unprepared for the size of the cavern from which the river flowed. The mountain loomed above, already snowcapped, reflected in the still black water of the winter river. Here if anywhere I could see, drawn by the hand of nature, the truth that it was all one. Earth, water, and sky lay together in unbroken harmony. It was like the moment at Terayama when I had been given a glimpse into the heart of truth; now I saw heaven's nature revealed by earth.

There was a small cottage at the river's edge just before the bird-perch gates of the shrine. An old man came out at the sound of the horses, smiled in recognition at Makoto and Hiroshi, and bowed to us.

"Welcome, sit down, I'll make you some tea. Then I'll call my wife."

"Lord Otori has come to collect the chests we left here," Hiroshi said importantly, and grinned at Makoto.

"Yes, yes. I'll let them know. No man may go inside, but the women will come out to us."

While he poured us tea, another man came out from the cottage and greeted us. He was middle-aged, kind, and intelligent-looking; I had no idea who he was, though I felt he knew me. He introduced himself to us as Ishida and I gathered he was a doctor. While he talked to us about the history of the caves and the healing properties of the water, the old man went nimbly toward the entrance to the caves, jumping from boulder to boulder. A little way from it a bronze bell hung from a wooden post. He swung the clapper against it and its hollow note boomed over the water, echoing and reverberating from inside the mountain.

I watched the old man and drank the steaming tea. He seemed to be peering and listening. After a few moments he turned and called, "Let Lord Otori only come thus far."

I put down the bowl and stood up. The sun was just disappearing behind the western slope, and the shadow of the mountain fell on the water. As I followed the old man's steps and jumped from rock to rock, I thought I could feel something—someone—drawing toward me.

I stood next to the old man, next to the bell. He looked up at me and grinned, a smile of such openness and warmth it nearly brought tears to my eyes.

"Here comes my wife," he said. "She'll bring the chests." He chuckled and went on: "They've been waiting for you."

I could see now into the gloom of the cavern. I could see the old shrine woman, dressed in white. I could hear her footsteps on the wet rock and the tread of the women following her. My blood was pounding in my ears.

As they stepped out into the light, the old woman bowed to the ground and placed the chest at my feet. Shizuka was just behind her, carrying a second chest.

"Lord Otori," she murmured.

I hardly heard her. I did not look at either of them. I was staring past them at Kaede.

I knew it was her by the shape of her outline, but there was something changed about her. I did not recognize her. She had a cloth over her head and as she came toward me she let it fall to her shoulders.

Her hair was gone, her head shorn.

Her eyes were fixed on mine. Her face was unscarred and as beautiful as ever, but I hardly saw it. I gazed into her eyes, saw what she had suffered, and saw how it had refined and strengthened her. The Kikuta sleep would never touch her again.

Still without speaking, she turned and pulled the cloth from her shoulders. The nape of her neck, which had been so perfect, so white, was layered with scars of red and purple where her hair had burned her flesh.

I placed my damaged hand over it, covering her scars with my own.

We stood like that for a long time. I heard the harsh cry of the heron as it flew to its roost, the endless song of the water, and the quick beating of Kaede's heart. We were sheltered under the overhang of the rock, and I did not notice that it had started snowing.

When I looked out onto the landscape, it was already turning white as the first snow of winter drifted down upon it.

On the banks of the river the colts were snorting in amazement at the snow, the first they had seen. By the time the snow melted and spring came, their coats would be gray like Raku's.

I prayed that spring would also bring healing, to our scarred bodies, to our marriage, and to our land. And that spring would see the *houou*, the sacred bird of legend, return once more to the Three Countries.

AFTERWORD

The Three Countries have enjoyed nearly fifteen years of peace and prosperity. Trade with the mainland and with the barbarians has made us rich. Inuyama, Yamagata, and Hagi have palaces and castles unequaled in the Eight Islands. The court of the Otori, they say, rivals that of the emperor in splendor.

There are always threats—powerful individuals like Arai Zenko within our borders; warlords beyond the Three Countries; the barbarians who would like to have a greater share of our wealth; even the emperor and his court, who fear our rivalry—but until now, the thirty-second year of my life, the fourteenth of my rule, we have been able to control all these with a mixture of strength and diplomacy.

The Kikuta, led by Akio, have never given up their campaign against me, and my body now bears the record of their attempts to kill me. Our struggle against them goes on; we will never eradicate them completely, but the spies I maintain under Kenji and Taku keep them under control.

Both Taku and Zenko are married and have children of their own. Zenko I married to my sister-in-law Hana, in an only partially successful attempt to bind him closer to me in alliance. His father's death lies between us, and I know he will overthrow me if he can.

Hiroshi lived in my household until he was twenty and then returned to Maruyama, where he holds the domain in trust for my eldest daughter, who will inherit it from her mother.

Kaede and I have three daughters: The eldest is now thirteen, her twin sisters eleven. Our first child looks exactly like her mother and shows no sign of any Tribe skills. The twin girls are identical, even to the Kikuta lines on their palms. People are afraid of them, with reason.

Kenji located my son ten years ago, when the boy was five. Since then we keep an eye on him, but I will not allow anyone to harm him. I have thought long and often about the prophecy, and have come to the conclusion that if this is to be my destiny, I cannot avoid it, and if it is not—for prophecies, like prayers, fulfill themselves in unexpected ways—then the less I try to do about it the better. And I cannot deny that, as the physical pain I suffer increases, and as I remember how I gave my adopted father, Shigeru, the swift and honorable death of a warrior, wiping out the insult and humiliation he had undergone at the hands of Iida Sadamu, the thought often comes to me that my son will bring me release, that death at his hands may be welcome to me.

But my death is another tale of the Otori, and one that cannot be told by me.

ACKNOWLEDGMENTS

I thank the Asialink Foundation, which awarded me a fellow-ship in 1999 to spend three months in Japan; the Australia Council, the Department of Foreign Affairs and Trade, and the Australian Embassy in Tokyo; and ArtsSA, the South Australian Government Arts Department. In Japan, I was spon-sored by Yamaguchi Prefecture's Akiyoshidai International Arts Village, whose staff generously assisted me in exploring the landscape and the history of western Honshuu. Thanks particularly to Mr. Kori Yoshinori, Ms. Matsunaga Yayoi, and Ms. Matsubara Manami. I am especially grateful to Mrs. Tokoriki Masako for showing me the Sesshu paintings and gardens and to her husband, Professor Tokoriki, for infor-mation on horses in the medieval period.

Spending time in Japan with two theater companies gave me many insights. Deepest thanks to Kazenoko in Tokyo and Kyushuu, and Gekidan Urinko in Nagoya, and to Ms. Kimura Miyo, a wonderful traveling companion, who accompanied me to Kanazawa and the Nakasendo and who answered my questions about language and literature.

I am indebted to Mr. Morgi Masaru and Mrs. Mogi Akiko for their help with research, their suggestions for names, and above all, their ongoing friendship.

In Australia, I thank my two Japanese teachers, Mrs. Thuy Coombs and Mrs. Etsuko Wilson; Simon Higgins, who made invaluable suggestions; my agent, Jenny Darling; my son Matt, my first reader on all three books; and the rest of my family, for not only putting up with but also sharing my obsessions.

In 2002, I spent a further three months in Japan at the Shuho-cho Cultural Exchange House. Much of my research during this period was useful in the final rewriting of *Brilliance of the Moon*. My thanks to the people at Shuho-cho, in particular Ms. Santo Yuko and Mark Brachmann, and to Maxine McArthur. Also, again deepest thanks to ArtsSA for a Mid-Career Fellowship.

Calligraphy was drawn for me by Ms. Sugiyama Kazuko and Etsuko Wilson. I am immensely grateful to them.

Turn the page for a rare interview with

Lian Hearn

AUTHOR OF THE
TALES OF THE OTORI

A Conversation with Lian Hearn

Lian Hearn, the pseudonymous author of the Tales of the Otori, prefers not to give interviews. However, Alisa McCune of the SF Site (www.sfsite.com) was most persuasive, and here are the fascinating results.

What is your background? How does it have impact on your writing?

I was born in England and [have since] emigrated to Australia. I think the main influences on my writing were my rather disturbed teenage years (I won't go into details) and studying modern languages (French and Spanish) at Oxford. I love languages and words: to learn a foreign language is to enter into a love affair with a country and its culture. It is to become a different person and begin to think in a different way.

Coming to Australia brought me closer to Japan, a country I had been interested in for many years. Australia has many links with Japan and is in the same time zone, though a different hemisphere. Being an Australian means being between West and East and living in a society that has formed itself out of many different and contradictory elements. I identify with this.

What drove you to become a writer?

For as long as I can remember I have been a storyteller, making up stories to entertain or console myself. I've always loved reading and wanted to write books that would enthrall the reader in the same way I have been enthralled.

What are you currently working on?

I am researching a long-term project to write a historical novel (not a fantasy) set in western Japan in the mid-nineteenth century.

Will there be any more books in the Tales of the Otori series after **Brilliance of the Moon***?*

I am writing two more: a sort of prequel which tells the life of Shigeru from age twelve until his rescue of Takeo in Mino and a final one which takes place fourteen years after the end of *Brilliance of the Moon*. I wrote all the first three books out by hand before I typed up *Across the Nightingale Floor*, and I am doing the same with these two, as the stories have to echo each other.

What kind of research did you do for the series?

I started to learn Japanese first. . . . I can speak a little and read quite a lot. I received a fellowship from Asialink, the Australian foundation which encourages artistic and cultural exchanges between Australia and Asian countries, to spend three months in Japan in 1999 and 2000. During these periods, I spent some time in western Honshu, which provides the landscape for the series. I have made many other trips to Japan as well in the last ten years, since I first had the idea of the story and characters. I went to museums, old temples, and other buildings; watched many movies; and read many books, including Japanese literature and poetry. And walked endlessly through rural Japan reflecting on its history and character. My way of gathering material is very intuitive: I steep myself in it and then forget the research while I write the stories, using details to bring the world to life.

The Tales of the Otori series appears to be an Arthurian-type story set in a medieval Japan. What inspired you to create this world and series? Why did you pick a Japanese-like location?

It's interesting that people see it as Arthurian as that was not a conscious choice of myth: many of the elements that seem to be Arthurian (the sword, the lost son, the blind woman) are also part of Japanese legends. Of course, I am a Westerner, and the myths that I internalized as a child are Anglo-Celtic. But I did not pick a Japanese location as such: it was more a question of being in the location and knowing a little about the history, and the characters and the story coming to me and grabbing me. In fact, it was rather a terrifying idea: I did not think I was in any way qualified to write from another culture, and I was filled with doubts and misgivings about attempting it. I tried to deal with this by setting the story in a fantasy world, but when I was writing, one of my main concerns was to be true to the culture that had inspired the fantasy and not to allow the characters to act in ways that they might not have done historically. I think this gives a certain realism to the fantasy.

The Tales of the Otori series has themes of love, betrayal, familial honor and honor as a warrior, death, and revenge. These seem to be prevalent in Japanese literature. Why did you decide to focus on these issues?

These are themes that recur in *Kabuki* drama and in the many Japanese *monogatari*. As I was writing, these were the ideas that my characters seemed to be concerned with. I was writing about a feudal society with all its codes and restrictions. My characters are forced into types of behavior by the society they are in: their reaction to this coercion drives the plot. But I did not want to write about "good" and "evil" and the struggle between them. The struggle in Tales of the Otori is between human individuals who seek power. I think the character of Arai is a good example of this. Arai starts out as a hero and champion of Kaede, but his ideas for her future end up being quite different from what she wants. And his drive for power leads him quite naturally to betray Takeo (or outwit him to use a less loaded term). And even the "good" characters are driven to perform shameful acts which they bitterly regret.

One issue never resolved in the series is whether peace can be attained and maintained without violence. What are your thoughts on this issue?

This is one of the key themes of the books. Takeo, who has been brought up with the belief that it is wrong to kill another human being, finds himself adopted into the warrior class, whose sole purpose is fighting and killing, and then taken into a secret society of assassins. He can join them or die himself. He always chooses to live, at great cost to his own emotions and soul. At the end of *Brilliance of the Moon* he takes upon himself the responsibility all states take: to control violence for the sake of all their people. The book I am writing now looks at how successful he is in this.

Takeo is such a strong, heroic figure. Was he based on anyone specific? How did you decide to create the mystery of his heritage with the Otori, Hidden, and Kikuta?

He is not based on anyone specific, though he may have elements of some historical figures. I am interested in flawed, gifted people with divided and vulnerable natures: his character just seemed to develop from that. I was also interested in the balance between compassion and ruthlessness that a feudal leader must need, and also in the way Japanese tradition combines the artist and the warrior.

In Grass for His Pillow, *Takeo has a sexual relationship with one of his closest male friends. Why did you decide to add this to the story?*

Like most young men Takeo has a strong sex drive and is susceptible. And, like most humans, grief sets desire alight in him. One reviewer wrote about the "matter-of-fact eroticism" of the series being true to the spirit of medieval Japan. Again this was where I was trying to let my characters live in a historical world. Strong attachments between young men of the warrior class were very common: their sexual nature was not an important issue. Fidelity in marriage was also not expected of men, though women's jealousy was recognized and validated in many plays and stories, and I felt this gave a plausible basis for Shigeru's pledge to Lady Maruyama.

The Tribe seems to be a ninja type of group. Is this intentional?

The words *samurai* and *ninja* have become somewhat clichéd in Western ideas of Japan. I wanted to avoid using these words and also to avoid romanticizing either of them. So the Tribe has skills that are all based on *ninjutsu*, but they are also moneylenders and merchants, extremely pragmatic and cynical.

The Hidden have aspects of early Christianity in their actions and religious practices. Why did you make them outcasts? Are the Hidden an early form of Christianity?

The Hidden come from two separate strands of Japanese history. One is the "hidden Christians" of the seventeenth and eighteenth centuries who were severely persecuted but who emerged in Meiji Japan (only to be imprisoned again) with vestiges of their faith intact. My story is set just before the first Westerners arrive in the Three Countries, and my Hidden are the remnants of a Nestorian type of Christianity, which might have come from China hundreds of years before. The Hidden are not outcasts as such, but many outcasts are Hidden, because of the appeal of a belief that holds all people are equal in the eyes of their Creator.

Kaede is another amazing creation. She is both strong and feminine at the same time. She can be impetuous, and yet she loves her family and Takeo with her entire being. What was the inspiration for her character?

Kaede is my tribute to all the Japanese women who are nameless in Japanese history, who figure in samurai family trees simply as "onna"—woman. And to my Japanese women friends who have little resemblance to the fragile Madame Butterfly type. But for all Kaede's strengths I wanted to show her realistically, constrained by a feudal, patriarchal society. She thinks she is riding into battle in *Brilliance*, but, even though she is armed, when it comes to fighting her physical strength is no match for a man's. The books contain a lot of unspoken references to the yin-yang nature of the universe, the balance between the masculine and the feminine. Kaede has to be strong according to her female nature. The love between her and Takeo is the balancing force that will bring peace to the Three Countries. Their marriage is a matter not only of romantic love but also of metaphysics, as well as, more mundanely, good strategy in war.

At the conclusion of **Brilliance of the Moon,** *Kaede is horribly scarred on her neck and back. I thought this was an interesting place for scarring, as in Japanese culture the nape of the neck of a geisha is considered a very erotic notion. Was this intentional?*

Yes, the scarring of the nape of the neck is intentional: it is such an erotic part of the body in Japanese culture.

What inspires you to write?

It's the way I understand the world, as well as an addictive pleasure, to create a whole world and people who have not existed before and to discover their stories.

Do you attend any writing groups? If so, how did your participation enhance your writing?

I am a very secretive and isolated writer and never show my work to anyone or even talk about it when it is in progress. It's both a strength and a weakness, I think. The strength is that the voice emerges strong and original; the weakness is in being cut off from other writers and what is going on in one's field. But then I don't really feel as if I have a field.

What made you a science fiction, fantasy, and horror fan? What are your favorites and why?

I can't really describe myself as a science fiction or fantasy fan. I hardly read anything in these genres. I'm a great admirer of Diana Wynne Jones, but I haven't read her latest books. I like J. G. Ballard too. And another favorite author is Haruki Murakami.

What do you enjoy doing when not writing?

I like being outside, doing physical things. Walking, swimming, kayaking, bird watching.

Any movies you particularly enjoyed?

I think my all-time favorite movie is Kaneto Shindo's *The Black Cats from the Grove—Yabu no naka no kuroneko*: It's a stylized ghost story, very moving and sad. The moment when the husband meets his ghost wife is sublime.

Has anyone optioned the Tales of the Otori?

The film rights to the trilogy have been bought by Universal for Kennedy Marshall. The script is being written at the moment by David Henry Hwang. It's exciting, as Kathleen Kennedy and Frank Marshall are such great producers.

ALISA McCUNE discovered science fiction at the tender age of eight. She devoured The Chronicles of Narnia by C. S. Lewis and never looked back. She lives in Chicago with her husband, cat, and five thousand books. For more information, please visit her Web site at **alisaandmike.com**.